G R JORDAN

The Numerous Deaths of Santa Claus

A Highlands and Islands Detective Thriller

First edition

ISBN: 978-1-914073-06-9

This book was professionally typeset on Reedsy.
Find out more at reedsy.com

Contents

Foreword

This story is set around the prosperous city of Inverness in the north of Scotland. Although set amongst known cities, towns and villages, note that all persons and specific places are fictional and not to be confused with actual buildings and structures which have been used as an inspirational canvas to tell a completely fictional story.

Acknowledgement

To Susan, Harold, Evelyn, Pete, Joan, Wendy, Jean and Rosemary for your work in bringing this novel to completion, your time and effort is deeply appreciated.

Novels by G R Jordan

The Highlands and Islands Detective series (Crime)

1. Water's Edge
2. The Bothy
3. The Horror Weekend
4. The Small Ferry
5. Dead at Third Man
6. The Pirate Club
7. A Personal Agenda
8. A Just Punishment
9. The Numerous Deaths of Santa Claus
10. Our Gated Community

The Patrick Smythe Series

1. The Disappearance of Russell Hadleigh (Crime)
2. The Graves of Calgary Bay
3. The Fairy Pools Gathering

Austerley & Kirkgordon Series (Fantasy)

1. Crescendo!
2. The Darkness at Dillingham
3. Dagon's Revenge

Chapter 01

Carly was annoyed. It was Emma's fault that she had taken this job and the girl was nowhere in sight. *Be an elf*, she said; *bit of Christmas money*, she said. Carly had briefly met the man who was to be Santa and she had taken a dislike to him already. Although the man was over six feet tall and built like the proverbial brick house, he had given Carly the once-over like she was a prize turkey at Christmas and leering from behind that white beard, he had given her the creeps. There would be no Ho-Ho-Hoing about with him.

The elf outfit was ridiculous too. Carly could live with the pointy ears and green felt hat on her head, even with the smart green and red jacket and shoes with the curly, pointed ends. But the tights. This was a kid's grotto and the elves had been given sheer tights that barely seemed to cover any leg at all. It was a good job they had seen the outfits yesterday allowing Carly to grab some thick white tights. If she were going to stand in an outdoor grotto she would be as warm as she could.

Emma stuck her head into the ladies' toilets where Carly was standing in her gaudy outfit. The girl had those sad eyes on and Carly was beginning to feel angry.

'No bloody way are you getting out of this! Don't give me those eyes that say I'm sick. You're going to do this with me.

It was your idea after all.'

The first term at the University had been fun and Carly had become firm friends with Emma, but the girl was prone to get carried away, sign them up for things, and then get nervous at the last moment. There was no way Carly was doing this one alone. Not with Pervy Santa beside her.

'Has he asked you onto his knee yet?' laughed Emma. 'I reckon he switched the tights just for you. Surprised he didn't pop a wee thing in there for a laugh.'

'You're bad,' said Carly. 'All joking aside, it would not surprise me if he made a grab for your arse.'

'It's not my arse he wants, girlfriend. I think he likes his blondes. Can see him having a cheeky fondle.' With that, Emma pinched Carly's bottom.

'Shut up and get changed. We only have another ten minutes and we're on. I heard there's a queue of kids out there already.'

'Looked busy when I came in,' said Emma, taking off her coat and starting to change. 'I can't believe I have to change in here either. You'd think they could get some decent changing areas sorted. I mean they must have staff lock-ups.'

'They do but they are communal. There was no way I was getting my kit off in front of Pervy Santa.'

'I'm going to end up calling him that,' laughed Emma. 'How do you think he'd take it?'

'Probably turn him on. Just make sure you watch my back. You've got a strapping boyfriend to come and knock his lights out if he tries anything on you. I have no one.'

'And who's fault is that?'

'Piss off. I am not dating Neil Mackenzie. The guy's a geek. But seriously, watch my back. You can get Dave to come round if the guy gets too frisky.'

Emma laughed again. 'Dave? He'd probably watch.'

'That's awful. He's well into you, Emma. Are you seeing him tonight?'

Emma pulled her green jacket over her head and pulled on the thick white tights Carly had bought. 'Yes, I am, so don't wait up.'

'Wait up? Don't wake me up. I've never known someone be so loud in a bedroom.'

'Well, with the right man.' The girls sniggered before falling silent as the door was rapped.

'Are we ready, girls?' It was Mr Haskins, the owner of the garden centre whose Grotto the girls were about to be gainfully employed in.

'Just about.'

The door opened and the small figure of Dermott Haskins stepped in. He was dressed in a smart silver suit and Carly thought he looked more like a gangster than a garden centre owner. Emma was standing with her tights halfway up her legs, jacket on but her pants showing. She would not blush; Carly knew that but then again, maybe Haskins would not either. He was a little greasy.

'Good, good, nearly there, Emma. Now Kieran has been ready for about half an hour, waiting in the grotto. I thought we could get a photograph later of Santa's elves sitting on his knee for the papers. You girls wouldn't mind that, would you? And what's with the white tights? There's no real snow in the grotto.'

'It's still cold in there, Mr Haskins,' said Emma, almost flashing her eyes at him as she half crouched, still not fully dressed.

'It is but I do think the original tights look better. But too late for that. I did want to do a summer grotto, Santa on a beach, bikinis and Bermuda shorts. My wife said it wouldn't suit the kids. Maybe she's right, but it would get the Dads coming, eh?'

Carly laughed along with Emma but as soon as the man shut the door, they looked at each other, pretending to be sick.

'Come on,' said Carly; 'best to get it over with. If Pervy Santa's been sitting in that ice box for a half hour, he's not going to be able to function anyway.'

'Not until he sees his favourite elf.'

'Shut up. Let's go.'

Emma led the way out of the toilets and along a back corridor of the garden centre until they came to a door that led to a large, gravelled area at the rear of the main buildings. A large tent had been erected, the outside of which had reindeer, elves, and snowmen on it. Walking around to the front of the tent, Carly saw a queue of children and parents and did her best to smile as a small child pointed Carly out to her mum. The girls quickly slid inside the entrance to the tent.

'Shit, look at the lights in here.'

'I think it would be better if Santa's Elves don't swear,' said Mr Haskins. 'Now you can take a half hour at a time inside the grotto and then swap. One of you will control the queue out here and the other just take the kids through, make sure they get their toy and photograph on leaving. That reminds me—where is that bloody clown with the camera?'

Carly sniggered as Mr Haskins ran off and watched Emma defiantly walk over to the small fence that surrounded the grotto. The inside of the tent had a winding path laid out with winter scenes of penguins and snowmen that culminated at a small house with a wooden fence around it. As the elves, one of the girls would man the entrance to the house ensuring an orderly queue and a steady flow to the house, while the other would assist Santa inside. Emma was making sure she was on the queue duties first.

'No way, tart,' said Carly. 'I'm not going inside the house with Pervy Santa.'

'Don't you mean love den?'

Carly punched Emma on the shoulder. 'Stop it! I mean it; he's too creepy; it's not funny.'

'Look, Dave said he was popping his head in around now and if I'm in the house he'll not see me. He's hardly going to pay for a visit to Santa. At least out here he will be able to see me.'

'You're seeing him tonight, so what the hell's the difference?'

'I want to see if he likes my elf outfit. I could maybe wear it later and—'

'Stop! No details, okay. I have to wear this outfit too, and I don't want any image in my head of you altering this costume.'

'I think Dave might like a pointy eared babe on top of him. He likes that woman off Star Trek with the pointy ears. In fact, he said the other night . . .'

Carly was holding a hand up and turning her head away in a pose that she had displayed to Emma more than once before. 'Too many details, I told you. I'll go in the house if you stop telling me about your sex life.'

The speakers inside the tent began to blast out a rendition of 'Santa Claus Is Coming to Town' and Carly struggled to hear what Emma said next. No doubt it would be about how Dave did this or that to her and Carly did not want to know. She was no prude, but she was happy in her own love life, dead as it was, without having to experience that of other people.

A photographer burst through the front entrance to the tent with Dermott Haskins behind him, poking him forward with his finger. 'Get to the rear of the house and wait for Carly here to call you through for the photographs.'

The photographer was a man of nearly sixty and he did not like the way he was being treated, but Mr Haskins was not in a mood for complaints. 'Okay, girls, places please,' he shouted loudly, and Carly watched Emma give a little kiss to her, followed by a saucy hip movement. Mr Haskins was watching Emma's tease of Carly and she thought he was going to give a rebuke but then as Emma kept going with her exaggerated actions, he simply watched, smiling. Carly shook her head and walked off to the house where Pervy Santa waited inside.

Passing by the small, wooden fence, Carly walked the paved path before her. The garden centre had really gone for broke with this setup and for a moment Carly almost felt proud to be associated with it, and with the chance to put a smile on so many children's faces. But Pervy Santa was still inside.

Opening the wooden door, Carly peered inside and saw that Santa was sitting on board his sleigh but was slumped at the reins. Two reindeer, one with a red nose, stood in front of the sleigh, and although plastic, in the dim light they certainly looked real enough. A stack of presents was in the rear of the sleigh and Carly remembered that boys were on the right and girls on the left, each section increasing in age by two years as they went back from the front seats of the sleigh.

'They're coming, Kieran.' Pervy Santa did not move, still slumped backwards. Maybe this was a trick designed to get her closer to him. Maybe he would feign death to force her to give him the kiss of life. How awful would it be to place your lips on this guy?

'I said they're coming, Kieran.'

Again, there was no movement. Was this just a plan to grab hold of her as she neared him? There was no reason to say he was out to get her. The man just looked pervy. Carly swore he was almost drooling when he saw Emma and herself the first time. But then maybe she was just imagining it all. He was married after all. But the magazines said that married men were the worst, especially for being forceful.

Enough Carly, just enough, she thought. Carly walked up to Pervy Santa and touched his shoulder, expecting him to jump up and make a funny comment. But there was nothing. No movement. Not even a grunt.

'Come on, Kieran.'

Despite the music, Carly could hear the sound of running feet entering the tent along with cries of delight. Inside a minute, someone would be here to see Santa and so far, the festive bringer of gifts was looking like he had drunk too many sherries. This would not be good. Hopefully, Emma would have the wit to check if everything were okay before she started shuttling the little ones inside. Then again, she was probably looking out for Dave. He was a nice guy and all that, but she never shut up about him. Or her sex life with him.

Carly put a hand on Kieran's shoulder and began to shake him gently. Again, there was nothing and she swore she could smell drink off him. That was all they needed—a pissed-up Santa. Still, that was not her problem and if he kept his hands to himself, she really could not care less what state he was in.

'And here's my friend, Carly. She's one of Santa's head elves too and she'll be taking you to meet with Santa who . . . seems to be having a lie down at the moment. Well, he has travelled all the way from the north pole.' Carly's head shot round and produced a smile that could have adorned a toothpaste commercial. But like those smiles, it was false.

'Santa's just going to be a moment, kids,' said Carly and again gave Kieran a small nudge.

There were four kids in the party that had come through the door to Santa's grotto and they had a parent with them who did not look impressed. Carly continued to smile until her gentle shaking of Kieran brought no response and so she mounted the sleigh and stood beside Kieran grabbing his shoulders forcefully. She shook him hard and then struggled to hold him as he slid towards her. Grabbing his top, she tried to hold on, but he fell into her and together they tumbled off the sleigh onto the grotto floor. Carly tried to recover herself and knelt beside Kieran but found that the man's eyes were open and staring blankly.

Had he had a heart attack? Was he in a coma? Had the booze simply got to him? There was a definite whiff of alcohol in the air. Then, to Carly's horror, one of the kids ran up beside her and stared at Kieran sprawled on the floor. The girl screamed loudly. She tore off to the entrance of the grotto and threw open the door. The child was only five or six but with tiny lungs at full volume, she shouted out to the excited throng in the tent.

'Santa's dead! They killed Santa; the elf killed Santa!'

Carly wondered what to do and then remembered her first aid. She had never used it but with a determined effort, she checked for pulse. None. Was his airway open? It seemed so. Was he bleeding? No, he wasn't.

At that point Mr Haskins ran in and nearly collapsed at the sight. 'Oh shit,' he shouted loudly. 'Not Santa, not Santa on today of all days.'

Carly looked at the man before her and as she started to perform CPR on him, ignoring her reservations of her mouth meeting the mouth of Pervy Santa, she realised that this festive season was going to be like no other for her. For she had killed Father Christmas.

Chapter 02

Macleod hugged Jane tight as he stood on the doorstep of their house. She had always had welcoming and warm arms but since she had been assaulted in her own house the way she held him had changed. There was more of a desperation, more of a cling rather than an embrace. And he could not blame her. If it had not been for Hope's intervention, he would have lost her, and in a truly horrible way. Jane would have been bathed in hot oil. But Hope had intervened, and he still had his Jane.

'Hazel's still here, and I'm on the mobile if you need me. Things will improve, you will feel safe again. Trust me.'

'You know I do,' said Jane. 'It's not you that scares me.'

'And they'll be changing the bathroom and the back room this week. You can start afresh.'

Jane nodded as he held her to his chest. 'This was ours, Seoras, our place. He changed that.'

'We can move if you want, I did say. Whatever it takes, you know that.'

She looked up at him and smiled. 'Maybe if I had Hazel's determination, her hunger to kick back.'

Macleod looked over Jane's shoulder at his friend and former forensic investigative lead. Hazel Mackintosh had suffered in the last investigation too, having been crucified at the castle on Loch Ness. Macleod had run to her, saved her, but his eye had been taken off the ball to the real target.

'This is about you. And there's plenty in Jane to come out fighting.' Wrapping her up tight again, he ran his hand through her hair. Dear God, he hoped she could turn this around because seeing her like this was killing him.

A car horn beeped and Macleod slowly released the grip on his partner. 'Got to go.'

'Another body?'

'There's always another body.' Macleod half smiled and turned away. Walking to the end of the drive, he took a glance back and saw Hazel with her hands on Jane's shoulders. It was such a turnaround from a few months ago when Jane had supported Hazel. Another beep made him turn back to the waiting car.

'I'm not that slow that I need a beep,' said Macleod, sliding into his passenger seat.

'I thought you needed help. I doubted you would be able to leave without a push.'

There was no sense of humour in the comment and Hope gave a brief wave at the two women in the doorway. The car pulled away and Macleod felt a wave of relief. Maybe he should not be glad to be away, but he was finding supporting Jane to be the most taxing thing he had ever done. Maybe he was selfish, looking forward to getting back into investigative mode. It was just a pity someone should have to die for him to find a release.

The car left the Black Isle and picked up the A9 towards Inverness. As they crossed over the Kessock Bridge, the domineering structure over the Moray Firth, Macleod was hit by the winter sunlight, low in the sky and something he hated when driving. Hope seemed unmoved by it but then again, she was wearing a large pair of sunglasses. Beside them, on her cheek, he saw the scar from the oil burn. It was obvious, a blunt statement of abuse that made newcomers reel in shock, at least internally, even if they could control their outer reaction. He had heard the comments:

'Such a lovely woman, ruined.'

'Hard to see that in front of you all the time.'

'How does she stay so emotionless when she looks in the mirror?'

'Something wrong?' asked Hope.

'No, nothing.'

'Then stop looking.'

Macleod went to complain that he wasn't or that he was only sympathising and then he realised the correct response. 'Sorry. How's things?'

'Fine.'

'Really?'

'Really!' Hope lifted her shoulders as she spoke, and Macleod could see the tension in her.

'Have you been trying any sessions with Jona, the mindfulness stuff she's been doing with me?'

'Apparently, I'm too distracted when I get her available. She's been up with you and Jane.'

Macleod turned back and looked out of the windscreen. Jona, the young Asian forensic lead had bonded with Macleod as a friend and the pair had been meditating together. There was a serenity to the woman and Macleod needed someone at the moment to help him let the pressure soak away. But Jona was also Hope's flatmate and they seemed to be having some difficulties. Jona had spoken to Macleod about them at their meditations but he could not bring that up here. Having someone to share with in Jona was great but confidences made life awkward too.

'Did you go with Stewart to her MMA class?'

'Are you my dad? Is this some sort of checklist?'

'Hope, we're just worried about you?'

'We?'

'All of us on the team. Stewart says we're a family, and she's right. You took a hit, so we're here for you.'

Hope flared her nostrils but remained quiet. After a short silence, she said, 'I went to the class. Afterwards we had a fight in the octagon. Stewart said it would be good for me to let off steam.'

'Was it?'

'I left more frustrated than going in. So, you figure.'

Macleod was intrigued. Surely a bit of exercise would let Hope blow away some anger. 'I think it didn't. But why?'

'She kicked my arse, Seoras. I couldn't focus, couldn't execute. Can't even fight now. What's anyone going to see in me?'

Macleod was no counsellor and he had tried to refer Hope to the various services available to her from the Police force, but she had refused. There was a stubbornness in Hope, a pride. At times it was extremely attractive but right now it was damn idiotic.

What's anyone going to see in you? thought Macleod. He had seen plenty in Hope and if he was twenty years younger . . . , well, who was he kidding. Just an old man's fantasy he had fled from because it was not good for working with his colleague. But he had always thought of her as someone who could be independent, able to stand alone. But Hope was not; she needed that support, that lifting up. Unlike Stewart or Ross.

The garden centre coming into view ended any further conversation and as Hope pulled the car up to the front door of the centre, Macleod saw Stewart already organising people. Jona Nakamura and her team were on scene and Macleod acknowledged a nod from the forensic lead.

The garden centre was a vast operation, it seemed to Macleod. Gone were the days when you simply popped in for plants or garden tools. These days you could buy fish, an entire pool system, country food, a range of books and toys. And there was also the obligatory café, or coffee shop as they were now known. A little more up-market than the greasy spoons he had started with in Glasgow.

Before him he saw a brick building and a set of sliding doors. To the left, he could see the wooden frames where the rows of plants and trees could be found. The coffee shop was at the rear, a fact he knew because Jane enjoyed coming here and wandering around, a pastime that frankly bored Macleod. But over to his right was a new feature. A large tent had been erected, complete with Christmas décor on the outside. The doors of the tent were closed and he saw the occasional forensic officer enter.

'Sir,' said Stewart, 'I think Miss Nakamura wants to talk to you about the deceased. She's requesting you grab a suit and join her inside the large tent. I have the girls who found the victim in an office out back, as well as the manager and the owner. Uniform have been taking statements from customers who were around, looking for anyone suspicious and also movements in and out of the tent. Ross is looking at the

14

technical side, CCTV and that.'

'Good,' said Hope over Macleod's shoulder. 'Shall we, sir?'

Together they walked over to the forensic van where they were handed white coverall suits by a young man. Macleod watched him stare at Hope. It was not unusual for men to look at his Sergeant but the man was fixated on her face. Hope looked up and the forensic officer diverted his eyes quickly, but she had caught him looking at her scar. She gave no reaction but it must have stung.

'Let's get inside,' said Macleod.

The interior of the tent reminded Macleod of a film he had seen with Jane. Not a keen cinema goer, Macleod had been dragged along and he had watched a scene of Christmas cheer inside a shop. The amount of gaudy decoration and extended stories about Christmas characters had surprised but not entertained him. Here he saw the same. Christmas was meant to be about Bethlehem and Macleod struggled to get everyone's excitement at a fat man in a red suit, a commercial marketing tool devised by a drinks company as he saw it. Now the real St Nicholas, maybe that was worth talking about, even celebrating. Growing up on Lewis, neither was that popular, although it may have changed somewhat since his youth.

'Inspector,' called Jona Nakamura, breaking Macleod's train of thought, 'over here in the house.'

Macleod had almost missed the house in the tent of distraction. He saw a fake-fronted building, complete with lights and dancing figures and walked through the supposedly wooden door to a room inside. There, beside a sleigh, lay a man in a red suit with black boots and an enormous belly. A white beard had been pulled down from the face.

'I'm presuming, Miss Nakamura, that I'm not here because

15

he had a heart attack. I doubt Stewart would have disturbed me for that, so what's the story?'

Jona knelt beside the victim and pointed to his neck. 'Strangled, Inspector. As far as I can tell from the markings on the neck, and I will need to get him onto the slab at the station for better analysis, but definitely strangled. I think it wasn't with a rope or cord either. I'm thinking an arm. Like a sleeper hold if you know it.'

'You said strangled, not choked, correct?' asked Hope.

'Correct. Choking blocks the airway. Strangulation blocks the blood flow.'

'Wouldn't you need to be strong to do that?' asked Macleod. 'I mean our victim doesn't look that weak.'

Jona reached down and pulled up the red jacket the man was wearing. Macleod saw a tight abdominal frame. The suit obviously contained some padding for the illusion of a fat Santa.

'I think the term today is our victim was *ripped*, Inspector. He was in great physical shape, a body that's been trained. He was probably surprised, grabbed from behind and a strangulation technique applied. You would need to be reasonably strong and also trained. You could not do this as a one off, a passing amateur. Also, it's a little weird because if you wanted to kill him as a trained professional, you could break the neck or kill in a quicker fashion. That's why I said sleeper hold. It's more like a wrestling technique applied for too long.'

Macleod stepped closer, looking at the man. 'Any identification?'

'Not on him but he was an employee, so the manager has plenty of details. His name is Kieran Magee. I think Stewart has the gen, but he has several tattoos on his body which may give more clues to his hobbies or lifestyle. I'll be done in an hour or so, Inspector, and I'll get onto the post-mortem after that. But there's little doubt he was strangled in my mind.'

'How long would you have to strangle him for?'

'Depends, Inspector, how well applied the hold was.'

'But you said this is a wrestling technique, Jona, so they are not aiming to kill. So, what makes it a death sentence and not just a wrestling submission hold. Could it have been accidental?'

'I doubt it,' sniffed Jona. 'If it were held for about ten to twenty seconds then they would go unconscious. But to kill it needs longer, twenty seconds minimum, but to be sure maybe forty seconds to a minute at least.'

'So, some strong man or woman, holding tight for that time?'

Jona shook her head. 'You don't have to be that strong to do this. If you can approach from behind so they can't get you once the hold is applied, they are weakening quickly. Technique is everything with this. Strength only came into any initial struggles you would have in applying the hold.'

Macleod nodded and turned away looking around the room. He saw a number of heavy items that you could bludgeon someone with. If you could approach stealthily enough to apply this hold, you could slit the throat with a knife, or snap a neck as a trained killer. This type of hold would be in the person's DNA surely, part of what they do or had done in life.

As Macleod made his way from the house back out to the main tent, he heard the music playing, the jolly tune being sung by a child and he looked around for someone to turn it off. He saw Stewart enter at the door and shouted over.

'Can we kill the music, Stewart? Bit inappropriate to be singing about Santa coming to town when he's lying on the

17

floor dead.'

'Was waiting for forensics, sir, the switch is in the back of
the building. Pulling it would kill all the power in here. The
isolator is in this tent but they were checking the switch for
fingerprints. I'll get it off soon as.'

Macleod watched Stewart, dressed in a white overall, enter
the house to speak to Jona and then come back out. She became
aware he was watching her. 'Anything else, sir?'

'Do you know how to strangle someone?'

'Well, yes, we have a range of techniques taught when we
grapple at the gym. Why?'

'I think you might be the woman for this investigation. Our
killer might be a wrestler of some description and certainly
knew how to strangle and not simply choke.'

Stewart shoved her glasses back up her nose in a show of
delight, but Macleod saw Hope turn away. 'Of course, Stewart,
you'll be following DS McGrath's lead.'

'Of course, sir.'

As Stewart disappeared from the tent, Macleod grabbed
Hope by the arm. 'Listen, you have this investigation. You lead,
I'll oversee. You call the shots; you find me this killer.'

Hope glared back. 'Is this some sort of pity offering. Hope's
not feeling grand so let's give her something to boost her?'

Macleod grabbed Hope by the arm and dragged her to the
rear of the tent out of sight of everyone. 'I offer you help, and
you don't take it. I can't speak to you because you have this
stupid front up. I know you're hurting and I'm sorry people
can't see past your badge of honour for saving a life. But I need
to know you can still cut this. Otherwise go and do something
else, Hope, for your own sake. One day, you'll be a DI and you
can't simply crawl into a shell because you got a kicking. So,

get off your arse and get me a killer.'

Her eyes burned at him. He could feel the anger and fury that came with her 'Yes, sir!' But he was right. She had been the impressive woman, having to battle past people who had seen her as a good looker, probably sleeping her way up to the top. She was not—she was a damn good detective. But now she needed to understand she was more than her injury, her looks, her personality. And if she hated him for showing her that then the hell with it. He'd been gentle these last few months. It was time to kick her out of her morbidness, waiting for a man or woman to lift her up. And deep down he prayed he was right.

Chapter 03

Macleod followed Hope to the main building where the restroom for the staff had been taken over by the police team. In a corner of the room beside a water fountain, two young women were sitting, dressed as elves. The comic nature of the surroundings of the murder was not lost on Macleod but it was dampened by the coldness of the killing. He watched Hope take a seat in front of the girls and stood back several feet as she began to question them.

'I'm DS McGrath and behind me is DI Macleod. I believe you were the people who found the body.'

One girl nodded and Macleod was aware that this woman was half staring at Hope's face while the other seemed a mess. 'Carly was the one to find him,' said one girl. 'I'm Emma, and we both work here for the seasonal stuff.'

'Where do you normally work?' asked Hope and Macleod saw her inadvertently turn to one side as if hiding her facial scar.

'We're students up at the university but we need the money, so we do this. Don't we, Carly?' Emma elbowed her friend, but Carly was still staring off into the distance.

'And you got employed here, how? Advert?'

'There was a job advert in the university magazine, the

weekly one. Nothing fancy, just looking for someone to be Santa's elves at various garden centres. So, we applied, came down here for an interview, which to be honest was more of a stand around in the costumes while the owner guy looked at you. And that was that.'

'Cash in hand?' queried Macleod from the rear.

'Exactly. But we don't care; it's not like I have any tax to pay.'

Hope was still sitting half turned away and she was clearly in thought. Macleod was ready with more questions but he decided to wait.

'Who actually employed you? Who gives you the cash?'

'That would be Gordon. I don't know his other name, but he was about here earlier. I saw him as I came in.'

'Where did you see him?'

'Just on the way in. We had to change in the ladies' toilets as the staff room is communal. I doubt many have to strip off and get changed for the other work here. But Gordon was passing me by as I came in. Carly was already here.'

'But where exactly did you see Gordon?' pushed Hope.

'In the staff area behind the main shop. We need to go that way to the ladies' toilets. Obviously, we changed in the staff ones, not the public toilets.'

'Can anyone vouch for that?'

'Yes,' replied Emma. 'The owner, Mr Haskins, popped his head in to see if we were ready.'

'He popped his head into the women's toilets to see if staff were changed?' echoed Macleod.

'Yes, he likes a bit of a look. In fact, he had given us a pair of sheer tights to wear, to show off our legs but Carly was not happy, so we have these thick, white, woolly ones. Bit more family orientated too, aren't they?'

21

'It was cold in the other tights.' Carly did not look at anyone as she said it, but Macleod could see tears welling up in her eyes. 'I only tapped him. I thought he was asleep, just drifted off and then when I pulled, he just fell. He was dead; you do see that he was already dead?'

'How long was Carly in Santa's House without you seeing her, Emma?'

'Not even twenty seconds. I came in with some kids that were overanxious, but Carly was trying to wake up Kieran. Then he tumbled off the sleigh.'

Carly stood at this point and looked right at Hope. 'I tried CPR; I tried to save him, but he was dead. Do you see? He was dead. The kid said that the elf had killed Santa, but I didn't. I didn't kill Kieran.'

Hope stepped forward to the girl. 'It's okay. Just take a seat and we'll get you out of here very soon. I just need to know a few things. And then tomorrow you can come into the station and give me all this in detail.' Turning to Emma, Hope asked, 'Either of you ever do any wrestling at university or anywhere else?'

Emma's face was a picture and Macleod reckoned the girl was fighting hard to not laugh. 'I never have, and I know Carly's never mentioned it. Kieran might have, he was extraordinarily strong. But he was also . . .'

'Also what?' asked Hope.

'Well, he's dead, so I shouldn't really say. But he was a bit of a creep. We hadn't met him much, but he was eyeing up Carly like anything in the tights she had at the interview. Taking a long look at us in the costumes.'

'Had you met him before the interview?'

'No, never. Neither had Carly. But from the start, he was

ogling, and not like Mr Haskins. Haskins accidentally drops in or has an awkward moment but it's all accidental. Kieran just stared. We called him Pervy Santa.'

Macleod listened to the rest of the interview impassively, but he thought the girls had little to do with the incident. They needed to get into Kieran's background and his other work colleagues who really knew him. When Hope sent the girls off to have their outfits taken by forensics, Macleod gave her a supporting smile, but he was unsure how she took it.

Dermott Haskins was in his office and McGrath and Macleod were led to it by a rotund older lady with glasses. She had the abruptness of a busy secretary and while always polite, she gave the impression that they were disturbing the efficient running of a garden centre. If they had not known, they would hardly have guessed there had been a murder.

Hope entered Haskins's office and strode to his desk to shake the man's hand before sitting down in a leather chair before she was even asked. Macleod liked this and took up a standing position near the door.

Haskins was a diminutive figure of a man, only around five feet six, but he seemed to have a bucket of personality. His silver suit had a purple shirt underneath and Macleod reckoned he was a young fifty-year-old or thereabouts. The dark hair on top had gel in it but not to the point where he looked like a sixties' throwback.

'Mr Haskins,' started Hope, 'DS McGrath and DI Macleod. I believe our officers previously asked you for all the work detail you had on Kieran, our victim?'

'Yes, of course,' said the man, smiling but trying hard not to be too bright given the topic of conversation. 'Here's his records. Not a lot in there but it does have his address.' He threw over a brown paper file. 'I was going to ring his wife but one of your officers said you would be doing that.'

'Yes, sir, probably for the best. How long had you known Kieran?"

'Not long at all. Well, when I say not long, he has done the odd job like this. I have an outside company bring us temporary staff from time to time. Criminal rehabilitation they call it. All very low-level offenders, served their time.'

'And what crime had Kieran committed?'

'I'm afraid you'll need to tell me as I don't get to ask that. They get cleared for work, but it certainly was not violence and not anything to do with children. I stipulated that when talking with the company, given the type of job this was.'

Hope turned away slightly as Haskins appeared to stare at her. Hope had always been able to stare down any creep, but Macleod saw the lost confidence and the interview seemed to be paused.

'Do you know of anyone who would want to wish any harm on Kieran—remind me of his full name—, sir?' asked Macleod.

'Kieran Magee. And no, I don't. Like I said, barely knew the guy. He could give a decent 'Ho-Ho-Ho' at the interview and seemed good with the trial kids we had so I didn't need to know anymore. Got in a couple of lovely elves and away we went.'

'Do you have any wrestlers, or former wrestlers in your employ, sir?' asked Hope.

'No, not that I'm aware, Sergeant. What a strange question. Why do you ask?'

'It's not important, sir, just a line of enquiry we were looking at. Do you have any other employees here today from this company you used? I'm sorry I didn't catch their name.'

24

The man seemed to shrink a little but then recovered himself. 'It's more of a one-man outfit, charity of sorts. His name is Gordon Stones and I've had dealings with him for years helping him rehabilitate offenders back into society. It's good for my own company to give something back. And in truth they have been good employees on the whole. You get the odd one who doesn't get into the work ethic but nothing else untoward.'

'We'll need his address and phone number if you have it,' said Hope. 'Does he have any wrestlers on his books?'

'I wouldn't know.' The delivery was smooth, but the man flinched as the question was asked. Something was bothering him, something that was not obvious but the wrestler reference or maybe Stones was the issue. It was clear as day to Macleod and he wondered if Hope had picked up on it. That was the thing with Hope; she had good procedure, could follow the path once it was there but she did not have that nose that sniffed out and saw the really little things. Stewart did in a way but usually in a trail of numbers or patterns in cases. Hope was more the thorough plodding police officer, like Ross, if truth be told. If he could only teach her to be a suspicious and observant grump like himself.

'I'm afraid our forensics will be here for a while, Mr Haskins, and I'm not sure you'll have your Santa tent back for at least another day, if not two. Please make yourself available over the coming days. I believe some of your staff are helping with getting CCTV images for us—that's appreciated. You'll have plenty to do over the next days, sir, but please nothing sensational to the press and if any of your people are having difficulties do offer them some sort of counselling. We'll need a full statement from you when you can get to the station please.'

Hope stood up and shook Haskins's hand. 'Oh, and don't contact Mr Stones before we do. Just a matter of routine, sir.'

'Of course not.' Macleod opened the door, letting Hope walk out of the office, but Macleod went over to Haskins and offered a hand.

'And please, Mr Haskins, remember to knock before entering a changing room full of ladies. Sorry, did I say changing room? I meant toilet.'

Macleod saw the man swallow and hoped he had planted the fear of engaging with Emma and Carly in any fashion. Turning away, he quickly caught up with Hope who did not look back at him but snorted, 'Performing all right, Boss?'

'No need for that. Did you see it?'

Hope now turned and looked at Macleod. 'See what?'

'Wrestlers on his books, when you asked that.'

'It's a possible lead, and we'll get into Stones anyway as Kieran Magee's employer.'

'He flinched. Very subtle but he flinched. I'm not sure if it's wrestlers or Stones that made him flinch, but he did. So, drive that line, it'll come up with something.'

As they reached the end of a corridor and tried to open the door, someone pushed the other way, and they reached an impasse. Beyond Hope, Macleod could see a tattooed face in the glass and gently pulled Hope back. The door opened and a strapping man stepped through. His head was tightly shaven and he wore a black leather jacket. He grinned as he walked past, his frame large enough that Macleod felt slightly squashed.

'Come on, Gordon, they are letting us through.'

An older man followed, broad in shoulders but not as well

defined as the younger man. As he stepped past Macleod, the Inspector held out an arm.

'Gordon? Gordon Stones?'

The man spun and stared at Macleod. He almost sneered but held himself.

'Who's asking?'

'Detective Inspector Macleod, and this is Detective Sergeant McGrath. I've just been speaking to Mr Haskins and he dropped your name in the conversation. I think I'd like a wee word with you, please.'

'Trouble, boss?' asked the younger man and moved somewhat menacingly towards Macleod.

'Easy, Sonny. There's been a murder here today and the Inspector wants to ask questions. Pretty normal thing for a copper to do, so don't get all excited on me. That right, Inspector, normal enquiries?'

'So far, Mr Stones, so far. But they are enquiries into a murder so let's not play it down too much. But I doubt Mr—'

'King.'

'I doubt Mr King has anything to worry about.'

'Maybe we could all have a wee word together,' said Hope. 'Not a formal interview, just a wee discussion about your employee, Mr Magee.'

Macleod saw the face of Sonny King drop before he caught himself. The man was definitely the brawn and not the brains. But Stones was smooth if untrusting and nodded his head.

'Well, Mr Haskins has an office, that would be ideal,' said Hope, and Macleod thought she was almost like her normal self, playing off his words and actions. Maybe forcing her to the front was not the best plan. But that would have to wait; it was time to talk to Gordon Stones and his friend.

Macleod had to stop himself from laughing when he saw Dermott Haskins's face as Hope led Stones and King into the office and asked for Mr Haskins to leave. The men watched each other close and Macleod tried to catch the looks, but he only saw that of Sonny King, and it was a grimace. But there was a tension in the room. Maybe they did or maybe they didn't kill Magee, but one thing was sure, his death was breeding some sort of displeasure between these parties.

Hope sat in Haskins's chair behind his desk while Macleod swept some paperwork aside and perched on the desk. While Gordon Stones took the seat he was offered, Sonny King had clearly watched too many movies and stood impassively behind Stones's chair and folded his arms like a bodyguard in the latest Hollywood thriller. But something was up. Would they be able to get it?

'I'm sure you will be upset to know that one of your employees is dead, Mr Stones. I take it Kieran Magee was one of your employees; that's what Mr Haskins advised us?'

Gordon Stones shook his head and his eyes looked reflective. 'That lad did so much to get to where he is today, Officer. He started out on the rough estates and got himself into a lot of bother before being locked up. I'm sure that much will be on his record but since he got out, the boy's done really well. Holding down a relationship. In fact, they were only married a few years ago. Such a pity.'

'We're going to pay a visit to Mrs Magee, Mr Stones, so I would be obliged if you let us break the bad news to her. Someone will be along directly from here and she'll need to identify him formally.'

'I can do that for her, least we can do. Do you have any idea who or why someone killed Kieran? It seems strange to me.'

28

Stones was not grinning, but his face was less than sombre like he was trying too hard to be civil at a time when one would expect at least a little shock.

Macleod was about to speak when Hope began again. 'That's what we are trying to establish, Mr Stones. Outside of work, how well did you know him? Mr Haskins said that you are running a rehabilitation programme for former criminals. Were there any issues there, or with anyone else you may have known from Kieran's past or present?'

'I'll be honest,' said Stones and Macleod's ears pricked up. That statement was rarely followed by the truth. 'Kieran had a bit of a temper and an eye for the ladies. Maybe he got himself into bother with someone's wife or that.'

'Are you aware of anyone in particular?' asked Hope.

'I don't want to be indelicate, this being Mr Haskin's business and that, and he is also a client of mine, but I know his wife Eleanor likes to put it about a bit, especially with muscley-type chaps. Kieran certainly had the muscle.'

'But he was recently married, that's what you said.'

'And? Let's not be naive here, Officer. Newly married men or women can play around as much as someone who's been tied to another for many years. And Eleanor Haskins is a good-looking woman. Very pretty face.'

Macleod saw the slight shudder in McGrath. It was a comment not aimed at her and Gordon Stones was not referring to her in any way, but Macleod saw Hope take it on the chin like it was a direct insult. He waited a moment to see if she would continue but when the pause became a little overstated, Macleod jumped in.

'Did you ever see them together?'

'No, not in the way I think you're asking. What was your

29

name again . . . Macleod?'

'Detective Inspector Macleod and the officer you have been speaking to is Detective Sergeant McGrath. Please bear our names in mind in case anything comes to you after the interview, Mr Stones. What about you, Mr King? As one of Mr Stones's employees, you would probably be privy to a chance comment or that.'

Sonny King gave a blank stare. 'He's asking if you ever saw or heard anything between Eleanor Haskins and Kieran, Sonny,' said Stones.

'I saw nothing.'

Macleod was unsure if the man was quite simple or if he was just playing the brawny fool to perfection. 'So, you never spoke to Kieran about Eleanor Haskins?' asked Macleod.

'I wouldn't say that we had *men talk* about her, you know.'

'*Men talk?*' asked Hope.

'Yes, *men talk*. About women. You know.'

'I'm afraid I don't,' said Hope. 'What things did you talk about?'

'You know.' Sonny King was beginning to sweat, and Macleod reckoned it was less a secret he was hiding than having to admit something in front of a woman. 'About her legs and that. Her t—boobs. Her chest, yes, that's it, her chest.'

'You spoke about her figure,' corrected Hope. 'Were your conversations that shallow or did you talk about anything else? Maybe what she did? What she liked?'

Sonny King's face was blank. *If they ever bring the male gender to court to justify our existence,* thought Macleod, *please don't let Sonny King be our witness.*

'We'll need you down at the station to make proper statements later today or tomorrow morning,' said Hope, 'but just to clarify, were either of you in the Christmas tent today at any point?'

Both men shook their heads. Hope looked round at Macleod asking if he had anymore and he shook his head in the negative. After a brief handshake, the two men left and Macleod looked at Hope.

'You okay? You took his comment about Mrs Haskins's pretty face badly.'

Hope glared but then she began to soften. 'Did it show that much?'

'Only to me. He wasn't commenting about you at all; you do know that, don't you?'

Hope took a deep breath. 'Every look at me, I see them staring at my face. They used to stare and it never bothered me, but now . . . I guess I always took my ability to attract men for granted.'

'You'll still attract, Hope, there's more to you than a face. But where now? I can't solve your esteem issues but I can get my detective back into shape.'

'We have a widow to speak to, sir. I guess that should be our next step. Uniform will have told her by now but we should speak before the dust settles. See if there's anything untoward from that end.'

'Did you think it a little odd that Stones threw up the whole other woman thing so quickly.'

'Absolutely,' said Hope. 'There's something else there he's wanting to hide but it's not going to come to light easily. I think we'll see just how much of a straying man Kieran really was before we get too convinced that this is some sort of resentful love murder. Widow then station, sir. Get the team together for a debrief and see what Ross has come up with on access to the tent.'

Macleod nodded and let Hope sweep in front of him out to the corridor. At least she was starting to realise she had an issue. Quite how to get her past it, was something he did not have answers for at this time.

Chapter 04

Kieran Magee had not been a man of money; after all, he was appearing as Santa Claus in a grotto for Christmas, but Macleod was a little surprised at the house he had lived in. There was a small crowd of neighbours in the street watching the comings and goings of various police cars and the few media people who had already arrived despite the name of the victim not yet having been released. It was not unusual for the press to have found out in advance of the name being released but Macleod thought they could show a little more decorum.

Hope fended off the requests for comments as Macleod and she were let into the small, detached house. The building was less than ten years old and the sitting room in which the victim's wife was currently sitting was cramped with an inordinate number of books on shelves and a television that could belong to a movie house in the corner. The two pieces of seating were close together and Macleod thought anyone in here must generally be alone as the arrangement of the seats was neither optimal for chatting or for watching the television.

Kylie Magee, the new widow, was sitting in a pair of tracksuit bottoms and a loose jumper with her blonde hair tied up behind her. Her eyes were red, presumably from crying but she did not look particularly distressed as the two officers produced their credentials.

'Mrs Magee, I'm DS McGrath and this is DI Macleod. First, may I pass on my condolences for your loss? I'm sure this is a very trying time, but we do need to ask you a few questions.'

'Of course,' said Kylie and swung her legs off her seat and pointed to the smaller sofa across from her for the two detectives to sit on. Macleod took one look and thought how the pair of them would look trying to squash into what seemed to be an optimistic two-seater and decided instead to stand by the door of the room. Hope dismissed the uniformed officer who had been sitting with Mrs Magee and sat on the edge of the seat, trying not to sink into the enveloping cushion.

'As routine, Mrs Magee, I need to ask your whereabouts this morning when Mr Magee was at work at the garden centre. It's purely routine.'

'I was here, Sergeant. It had been a late night last night and Kieran had laid in with me. He had been slightly delayed as we had got a bit carried away in the shower and I then came downstairs when he left and was here until your officer came to the door. It was a bit of a shock. Well, at least in some ways it was.'

Hope sat further forward. 'How come? Obviously, you did not expect him to not be coming home, or did you?'

'Kieran was up to something in the evening. Well, not every evening but he was certainly in places which he did not want to tell me about. I had become a little resigned to it as, well, I have this house and I don't work. Kieran took care of me even if we didn't have the closest of relationships. Sure, it was all fun and games to begin but in the last year we have more learnt to share this house rather than be partners. So, forgive me if

I don't shed too many tears. He was a friend, yes, but lately the marriage had become more of an arrangement. I thought I should share that with you, so you didn't find it strange later on if it came out.'

Macleod saw his Sergeant glance over at him before Hope shook her head and the red-haired ponytail flopped about. Clearly, she was a little suspicious at the woman's admission, her jostling of her head was a dead giveaway, but he was interested to see how Hope would tease any more out of the woman.

'So, if you can run me through the times of this morning; what you did, when Kieran left. Also, if anyone saw you.'

The woman nodded and looked at the clock on the wall. 'It must have been about eight o'clock when he rose and I heard him get breakfast. He brought me some up too, nothing romantic, just a bit of toast. In fact, the plate is still upstairs on top of his. Then he went to the shower and I joined him because he had that look. We both still needed that side, Sergeant; it was part of the arrangement. And we enjoyed it together. It was no burden, if you understand—there just wasn't that kind of close connection people have who really want to be together . . .'

Macleod looked around the room and saw many photographs of Kieran and Kylie Magee. Most looked like the traditional couple pictures you would find in a lot of houses, certainly those where the children had not arrived and taken over as the subjects of the visual displays. The woman was being particularly frank, and this made a refreshing change for Macleod, but it also set off the doubts in his head. But then again, he seemed to have doubts when anyone spoke these days. The fact he had been right on so many occasions just

35

fuelled his suspicious mind.

'So, when your love making had ceased . . .'

'Sex, Sergeant, let's not overplay it. We came out of the shower around nine, nine fifteen. Kieran dressed and left. He was due to start at ten and we are only ten minutes away. He would have got there early but he wanted to be on time. In truth, he was a bit nervous about being Santa Claus. You can see he was quite a large man, very trim, well-honed. I don't mind telling you that was part of my initial attraction to him. But he's hardly a cuddly Santa figure.'

Hope coughed. 'So why was he playing Father Christmas?'

'The money, I think. He did some work for Mr Stones. You know that Kieran had a record, don't you? He came up from a broken home and got into drug abuse, but he was helped out by the program, the New Start or something like that. Mr Stones runs it. We would often get calls from Gordon Stones and he would advise Kieran where he was going to go. Been that way for a number of years. I'm not sure how it all works; you'd need to ask Mr Stones but I know it gave Kieran a regular income.'

'So, you have stayed in since Kieran left this morning and until one of our officers called to tell you the sad news of your husband's death.'

'That's correct.'

'Anyone see you?'

'No, I didn't get the post; it was still here when I opened the door to your officer. I'm sure they'll tell you that because I was picking it up just before I opened the door to them.'

Macleod watched Kylie Magee's face. The woman looked sad but not overwrought which certainly matched her description of the relationship she had with her husband. There was an element of shock and she had been very forthcoming, too forthcoming perhaps? Macleod mentally shook his head. Evidence first, Macleod. But he could not shake off the feeling he had.

'How did you meet?' Macleod just blurted it out and he got a scowl from Hope, deservedly so. He was meant to be letting her take the lead, was observing how she performed but as per usual his detective nose was getting in the way of his intentions.

'Was at a fight,' said Kylie quite casually.

'A fight?' queried Hope.

'Yes, an MMA fight in Glasgow. They ran a bus from up here down to it. I ended up sitting beside Kieran.'

'You went on your own?'

'No, there was a gaggle of us girls going, and I ended up on the odd seat. The others were pretty jealous as Kieran was in his muscle t-shirt. You see, Kieran was a big fan, always had been. He even trained here in the house, one of the back rooms has a wee gym he used. So, we went to the fight, watched all the matches on the card and he basically stuck close to me. On the way back on the bus we got it together and it basically went from there. We had a whirlwind romance for six months, got married, and then drifted apart about two years later. I don't think we had that much in common. I tried to go with him to more of the martial arts things and that, but he didn't go to my book clubs, or even read the books I bought him. Guess that's when we lost it.'

'But you stayed together?' asked Hope.

'Yes, more convenient. We had a discussion, and we were happy to. I've never been the one for a romantic ending.'

'This will sound insensitive, Mrs Magee, but I do need to

ask. With Kieran's passing, do you gain much from his will?'

'I doubt he has one,' said Kylie dismissively. 'As for gaining anything, this is it. We rent the house, so I'll need to get a job, not that I'll be unable. I haven't given any thought about whether I'll stay here but I'm in no hurry to get away. Everything else we own is in the house and it's not a lot. As far as I know Kieran only had one brother and he's dead too.'

'Really, how did he die?' asked Hope.

'I think it was to do with drugs. It was a few years ago and they found him at the edge of a road, beaten to a pulp. The police believed it was a drugs issue and he had been made an example of. David was his name, but he was Davie to everyone he knew. We saw him occasionally here, but he was not a regular visitor. In truth, I think Kieran was a bit embarrassed by him.'

'Was Kieran holding any grudges against those who killed Davie?'

'Not that I was aware of. Certainly, he wasn't actively trying to find them or get to them. He had decided to let it lie; that's what he told me. I was a little concerned that if he went and did something daft, they would come after me. But he didn't and I have never had any contact with any drug dealers or any of that sort. Davie should not have got involved.'

'Was there anything else in Kieran's life, anyone else who might want him dead?'

'No, no one I can think of. But, then again, his working life was a bit of a mystery to me. I guess you need to ask Mr Stones about that.'

'Okay,' said Hope rising, 'again my condolences for your loss. May we take a little look around. I doubt we'll find anything of note but it's just procedure.'

'Sure, look away. By the way I think your liaison officer is a bit over the top. I'll be happy just to get the circus away from my door as soon as you can. I'll be fine, just be a bit easier to say what goodbyes I have in private.'

Hope nodded and pointed out of the door, indicating to Macleod they should start their look upstairs. Once in the hallway of the house, Hope climbed the stairs to the two bedrooms on the first floor. One, although cramped, had an en suite and she saw the shower Kylie had spoken about. Sure enough, it was still damp inside. Running her eyes across the wardrobe and drawers in the room, Hope saw a few hair products, deodorants, and other hygiene items as well as hairbrushes.

Macleod stood and watched from the doorway before looking at the tiny back bedroom. It had a single bed and a few drawers but looked as if the room had barely been used and certainly not recently.

Making their way downstairs, Hope went to leave but Macleod pointed to the rear of the house and led her to the exercise room Kylie had hinted at. The room was clearly meant to be a dining room, adjacent to an open kitchen. But instead of a table and chairs there was a bar on the wall for pull ups, an exercise ball, a punch bag, and various weights. On one side was a neat modern chest of drawers and he pulled out the top drawer to find shorts and training tops. The second drawer had socks and underwear. But the third and last drawer had an array of female exercise clothes.

'So, our distant wife likes the gym too,' said Macleod.

'And what's wrong with that?' asked Hope. 'She looked in good shape, although it was hard to tell just how good because of the baggy clothes she was wearing.'

THE NUMEROUS DEATHS OF SANTA CLAUS

Macleod bent down to pick up some weights but found himself struggling. Brushing past him, Hope lifted a weight and then put it back down quickly. 'They're pretty hefty, aren't they?'

'There doesn't appear to be a great range, McGrath. I would have thought if Mrs Magee were working out here too, there would be a range of lesser weights.'

'Who says she can't lift these?'

'Well, you're struggling, McGrath, and you're in decent shape. I might be old and decrepit, but you can stay with most gym enthusiasts.'

'I'm more cardio than strength, sir. These are pretty full on. But if you were into weights then maybe you could lift them. I wouldn't rule out Mrs Magee using these.'

'And she could get close without him being suspicious. Think about it. You know, like me, that most murders are domestic. Maybe this is one of them. Maybe that's an act in there because it all sounded very convenient. And she's certainly not that bothered about his demise.'

Hope nodded but then looked about at the weights again. 'Too early to tell, sir. She's certainly not off the list but there's no evidence to say she was there.' Macleod raised his eyebrows. 'I know,' said Hope, 'there's no evidence to say she wasn't either. She's got no alibi. I'm just saying she's a suspect and nothing more. Just keeping things open.'

'Good,' said Macleod, and thought he sounded like some sort of patronising father. 'Sorry, what next?'

'I say we get back to speak to the team and see what the CCTV has pulled in and who could have done the deed. Once we have that, we can narrow down the enquiries because at the moment, we don't have any good reason this man's dead.'

Macleod watched her walk from the room, through the kitchen and then disappear, heading towards the front door. His eyes then swung from the equipment back to that third drawer. Something was bugging him. But there was no evidence to back it up, just instinct. The station it was. Time to share with the incident room.

Chapter 05

'Okay, team, let's have your attention. Time for the briefing.' Ross's voice calmed down the busy room and Macleod watched over the small crowd of uniforms and detectives from the side. Hope stood at the front with Ross and now took centre stage. Macleod knew he would have to finish off with a small impromptu speech which would galvanise the troops. They were unaware of the prominence Macleod had given Hope in this investigation and they would stay that way. Never would he let it be seen that he was assessing Hope, watching her performance after her serious injury.

'Right, a brief recap for those who are just coming on board. This is all pretty fresh and we are still pulling in information so listen up and listen well; a lot of this will not have been broadcast for your attention yet.'

Hope had started well, and Macleod always thought she cut an imposing figure from the front. Unlike himself, she had that stance which demanded attention. His was a more awkward, half slumped look as if he struggled to support the whole of his weight. He knew his reputation was one of a grumpy taskmaster but his record stood tall in terms of his detection rate. Hope was still very much in his shadow and many preferred to route bad news through her to him rather than receive his wrath, often unwarranted. But then, that's what a Sergeant was for.

'Our deceased is Kieran Magee, employed by a former criminal trust to various jobs, the latest being the part of Santa at Haskins's garden centre. During his first stint, Mr Magee was strangled, not choked, in a move that was precise and effective. Mr Magee is known to have an interest in mixed martial arts and was built like he could be part of the scene. He certainly worked out at home and also did other work for Gordon Stones who manages the Rehabilitated Offenders Trust.'

Ross stepped in front of Hope, passing out sheets of paper which contained photographs and various details of the victim and his known associates. 'You'll see on your sheets the names of everyone at the garden centre today, or at least those we have identified. Despite holding most of the customers and staff there initially, there may have been a few escaped our grasp before we got on scene. There's a television request out for further information.'

'Have these contacts been interviewed?' asked a uniformed officer.

'No, and that's what will be happening tonight. We have addresses and DC Ross will be organising you all to attend various homes for statements. Remember, we are looking to see who was around the Christmas tent prior to the murder and if anyone was seen emerging from it before the body was found.

'Mr Magee was found by his elf. Yes, no tittering. please; we have a dead man on our hands. Carly Forsythe is currently giving a statement but there's nothing untoward at this time to link her to the death other than being the unfortunate person who found our dead Santa. Her colleague, Emma Macintyre, is also giving a statement but they both say they saw no one enter or leave in the short time they were there. Unfortunately, they were rather tardy to their positions and it seems Mr Magee was in the tent for a good twenty minutes on his own, or at least before someone strangled him.

'DC Ross will now give you a rundown of some of the main players at the centre.'

Ross stood up as Hope stepped to one side. In his hand was a red laser pen and he nodded at Stewart who flashed an image on the screen behind him.

'Evening, everyone. Right, first up is Dermott Haskins. Some of you may know him, owner of the garden centre. You have his picture on your sheets. We know he was at the staff ladies' toilets not long before the girls arrived at the tent but prior to that he says he was in his office but has no alibi. We don't have any reason to suspect him, but he is a key figure who can move about the area easily and understands where all the CCTV is.

'One thing to note is that we do not have CCTV coverage at the rear of the tent and therefore, we don't have any footage of who entered from that position. The garden centre does have full coverage on its perimeter fences, so we know whoever was in there, was also on our CCTV footage. However, with hoods, tops and angles, we cannot identify everyone in there. It's fairly easy to move about inside the centre and avoid the cameras as most are in the product areas which the temporary Christmas tent was far away from. Hence eyes on the scene may be our best weapon.

'I'll be detailing a small group to search the CCTV and

thereby cross off anyone who was visible during the twenty-minute kill window in the correct areas so as not to have committed the murder. By process of elimination from eye witnesses, we may be able to cross off some more. Next, please, Kirsten.'

Ross watched as a picture of Gordon Stones came onto the screen. 'This is Gordon Stones, former detainee at her majesty's pleasure but now the driving force behind the Rehabilitated Offenders Trust. He has hinted at some issues between Kieran Magee and Dermott Haskins, but nothing was substantiated. And this figure,' Stewart reset the picture, 'is Sonny King.' There were a few whistles. 'Yes, bit of a specimen and quick to the fist if the boss's encounter with him today was accurate, so tread carefully if you come into contact. We're not sure if anyone has any real beef with Kieran Magee but so far these are the only three people at the scene we can connect to him in any way.'

'Was his wife there?'

Hope stepped forward, holding a hand up to Ross. 'She says not, and we have nothing to say any different.' An image of Kylie Magee flashed up behind Hope. 'Thanks, Stewart. If anyone saw this woman at the garden centre, then that is big news and we need to know, so show her picture. Get a description and then show it—let's be thorough.

'We play this by going through all our witnesses and seeing if anyone can tag a suspect to the tent. We also drive at Haskin's Garden Centre and see if there's anything untoward there. Get an insight into the Reformed Offenders Trust. So far, we have nothing, no one who wanted our Santa dead. Given the manner of the death, it's unlikely to have been a random or chance effort. So, dig and find me the connections.

'Stewart will handle the technical investigations, looking into bank accounts and other sides to business and personal accounts. Ross will take the visual observations and all interviews. Be aware that the one thing we know is our man was strangled, not choked. This was done by someone who had a knowledge in what they were doing. They did not throttle him, simply wrapped the arm around from behind and precisely cut off the blood supply, not the air supply, similar to a wrestling submission hold. Anything of a wrestling nature, flag it up.'

Hope stepped away and opened a hand out to Macleod who slowly walked to the front of the room. Before he spoke, he observed the team before him. He knew most of them, some well but that did not matter. All eyes were watching and he pointed at Stewart who put the last picture up on the screen. Macleod shook his head and waved his hand indicating he wanted the first picture that had been up. The picture of Kieran Magee dominated the screen.

'Look at him. All of you look at him. He'd beat the head off me in a fair fight. I reckon he could take anyone here in a fair fight and probably beat them too. Maybe Stewart might manage him but not many others. And that's because she's been trained.

'So far we have nothing. Absolutely nothing. No one who hated him, no one who was even owed something by him. Yet someone, who he almost certainly knew, was able to come up behind him and hold him for at least twenty seconds and maybe more. Hold him in a precise hold to starve the brain of oxygen and kill Kieran Magee.

'Now we may not be looking for a professional killer, but we are looking for someone with training. A little bit of strength to maintain the initial hold and then clinical expertise to execute the killing hold. The press will be telling everyone Santa's dead, found by an elf. They'll ham it up and probably make a poor joke of it coming up to Christmas. But this was a calculated murder. But why?

'This will not be a pretty investigation. So far, we have nothing, so we dig up the dirt. Push hard at people and when it looks like someone is hiding something use whatever it takes because that is how we'll find out this one. It won't come from me, or the Sergeant, or Stewart or Ross. It'll come from your digging. So, get out there and dig. Someone killed Christmas for a lot of kids. Let's get this sorted before it becomes a festive joke.'

Macleod watched the faces before him and saw a sea of sullen complexions with determined eyes. The mood was right. 'And take care,' he added, 'there's snow coming and it's going to be a right blizzard for the next few days. Stay safe.'

Hope appeared beside him and shooed the team into action before pulling him to one side. 'Ross said the DCI was on the phone looking for an update just before we started.'

'Speak to her, Hope. I'm indisposed. She was impressed with you at Fort Augustus so make the most of it. She's usually hacked off at me. Says I'm a dinosaur, not like you new people.' Macleod grinned as he said it.

'I wish I had your instincts though. No one saw Fort Augustus but you.' Macleod went to hold up his hand, but Hope was right, and she did not deserve his feigned modesty.

'But I lack other things—speed, a delicate touch. You have so much, just find yourself a person with instincts, like I found Stewart to handle anything with a power lead. Like I found a steady hand in Ross to cover off the loose ends.' And now

47

he held Hope's hands. 'Like I found you to counter me, to challenge this old fart. I don't have everything, and neither will you. You need to find these things.'

'It sounds like you're retiring,' said Hope in a whisper.

'Maybe. Or maybe I can see someone who can run her own murder team and needs a shove to get up beyond me. I can't play the games, Hope. The DCI, she can. That's why she's up there and I'm still a foot soldier.'

'More like a centurion.'

Macleod wondered if she was making a joke of his age, but he let it pass and wandered off to make a phone call. The team were off and running and he wanted to give Hope some breathing space with her investigation. He could not watch her all the time; it would be suffocating.

When he returned to the room, it was a lot quieter as most of the team had gone out to interview the witnesses in their homes. But he saw Stewart with her arm around one of the team, imitating some sort of hold.

'Sorry, sir. I was just trying to show PC Davidson here what a submission hold looks like. Also, why it was a strangulation and not a choke.'

'How au fait are you with these moves?' asked Macleod.

'We do get trained on them at the MMA club but you need to be reasonably experienced to pull them off really well.'

'Can you do it?'

'Well, yes.'

'Could you have done it to Kieran Magee?'

'I believe so. It would be easier if he didn't know I was there.'

'Or if he trusted you?'

'Much easier then,' said Stewart.

'Can you cry out if this happens to you?'

Stewart looked a little unsure. 'Depends on how well it's done. You can be unconscious very quickly. And if they had stuffed something in your mouth at the same time, you wouldn't be able to alert anyone.'

Macleod nodded and waved his hand at others to carry on. Hope was seeing to a statement from Gordon Stones where he was simply signing off on a prepared comment he had made with his solicitor. But Macleod's attention was grabbed when Ross came at him waving a piece of paper.

'Sir, there was another rehabilitated criminal there as well, one Gordon Stones failed to mention but he would have known him. An Angus Fischer, resides in the town. I have a team interviewing him now. Apparently, he's not too keen on Mr Stones.'

'Okay, Ross, ask the Sergeant if she wants him brought in.'

'Sir?'

'You heard me, Ross, ask your boss.'

Macleod watched the bemused man walk away to find Hope and it occurred to him that letting Hope run the investigation was not going to be easy if everyone thought he was in charge. Oh well, so be it. He'd just have to be a grumpy old fart and let them blame it on his age.

But his mind returned to what Stewart had said and he stared at her from the side of the room. She was in good shape, had strong arms and was a bit of a pocket rocket but he never thought she could have held someone like Magee for that long. But if he was weakening right away, unconscious within seconds, then maybe yes.

Macleod lifted up a piece of paper from the desk in front of him and stared at Kylie Magee. That feeling was still there and now he had a possible way for her to kill her husband. He

49

wanted to storm round there and demand to see her muscles. Even if he put aside the deriding remarks he'd receive and the idea that most of the station would see him as some sort of deranged pervert, he knew it was not something he could get away with. Besides, it was not proof. But with so little to go on, his instincts were the best he had.

Chapter 06

Kirsten Stewart stared at the computer screen and shook her head. Together with some uniformed officers, she had started trawling through the records of the main suspects and by that it meant anyone who had a connection to Kieran Magee. Currently, she was looking into Sonny King, the impressively built former criminal who seemed to have less going for him upstairs.

One thing noted on Sonny's record was a tattoo for a gym in America. Stewart had recognised the fish head logo instantly as one of the most famous mixed martial arts gyms going and though she doubted Sonny would have ever been there, one would not expect a person to sport such a tattoo unless there was a connection to the sport.

Taking one of her regular punts, of which most failed, Stewart put two and two together and decided to look at the gyms in the area that had MMA attachments. The records for most were not online but she trawled through the pictures on the websites and looked at committee members and various other links from the pages. In the rear of a shot, she could see the shaved head of Sonny King, or at least someone who looked extremely similar. Reading the passage below the picture, she discovered a trainer by the name of Kurt Eiger was in the foreground of the shot.

'Boss!' shouted Stewart to Hope who was at the far end of the room. Stewart watched her colleague walk the length of the room and swing round behind her as she pointed to the man on the screen.

'Who's that?' asked Hope.

'Kurt Eiger, trainer at Spark's gym. I think I've seen him about at local fights. But the interesting thing to note is the man in the background. It's a bit blurred but it looks like Sonny King. Given the method of the killing, the gym might be worth checking out to see if Sonny had the necessary training to finish off Kieran Magee like that.'

Hope nodded and tapped Stewart on the shoulder. 'And you should go. You know the world better than any of us.'

'Shall I tell the Inspector?'

'Take him with you,' said Hope. Then Stewart saw Hope's face shy away for a moment before she corrected her statement. 'Sorry, ask the Inspector if he wants to go with you. If not, then take a uniform but tell them to go plain clothes.'

'Will do,' said Stewart and grabbed her jacket off the chair behind her. She found Macleod in his office.

'Can I help you, Stewart?'

'Yes sir. I've clocked a connection between a local MMA gym and Sonny King and was going to check it out. The Sergeant suggested that I ask if you wanted to come along. I know it's a routine enquiry, but she seemed to think it was a good idea.'

Watching her boss take a moment to think, she was surprised when he sprang from the chair and grabbed his coat. 'Let's go. I take it the gym will be pretty active at this time.'

'I would expect so, sir.'

'Then you'd better look after me. More your territory than

mine.'

With that he swept past her and headed for the car park with Stewart struggling to keep pace. The Inspector seemed somewhat buoyant which was not him at all. Even more surprising was when Macleod took the driver's seat, something he rarely did and especially not at night. As they pulled out of the car park, snow began to fall in a swirling blizzard. The wind was not overly strong but the effect it was having on the descending flakes made seeing any distance difficult. Despite this, Macleod was almost whistling.

'You okay, sir?'

'Perfect, thank you, Stewart. Just nice to get out and about. When we get there, I want you to run things. I'll chip in if needed but you take the lead. After all, you understand the terms and that.'

'Yes, sir,' answered Stewart but she was feeling a little bemused. Maybe it was the Christmas Spirit.

The gym was located on the edge of Inverness along the river and the car park was almost full. When they reached the door of the club, they found it locked by a keypad and Stewart banged on the door. Shortly, the door opened and a tall, mean, young man looked at them. Before he could speak, Stewart introduced herself and her Inspector and flashed her warrant card at the man's face. She then barged past him.

Exiting a short corridor, Stewart entered a room she understood well. In the middle was a small octagon with net walls and a sprung floor. There was an open door to it and inside a trainer was taking a young man in shorts with a bare torso through his paces. A few ladies were sparring on a mat in the corner while other fighters were training on various pieces of gym equipment. There was a quiet buzz that hushed as

53

Stewart and Macleod entered the room.

'Good evening, everyone. I'm DC Stewart and this is Inspector Macleod. We need to talk to Kurt Eiger if he's in the room. It's nothing untoward, just a chat for some information.'

The room should have started a short buzz, people questioning each other about why Mr Eiger was wanted by the police but instead there was a deadly hush. After a moment, a man stepped forward from the rear of the hall. He was at least six feet four and Stewart had to bend her neck to look at him.

'Do you have a warrant? Most of us have done this before and we know the score. If you don't have a warrant, then piss off as Mr Eiger will not be talking to you.'

'Why? All I want is a chat. Enquiries regarding a certain Santa Claus who's met his maker.'

The tension in the room increased and Stewart was wondering why there was such hostility. She could, of course, come back with more officers and try to get a search warrant if possible but there was no need.

'Go now, or I shall remove you for trespass, dearie.'

Did he just say, dearie? There's no way I'm leaving here without Kurt Eiger now. Stewart tried to step past the giant of a man, but he stepped across her path.

'I said leave.'

Stewart went to push on past, but the man reached out and grabbed her by the waist. He was strong but he had not got her off her feet yet. She drove an elbow into his stomach which merely surprised the man. He stepped back and then tried to drive a fist to her head. Stewart's own time training for the octagon made her take evasive action and she swung her head this way and that as the man threw more punches. As he overreached, she stepped aside him, grabbing a wrist and twisting the man's arm. At the same time, she drove hard into the rear of his knee causing him to fall to the ground. Her arm slipped around his neck as he went to his knees. The man's arms went out, flailing for her but then slowly began to weaken and within ten seconds he was lying on the floor struggling to recover.

'If Mr Eiger will kindly show himself, I won't press charges against this amateur.' The place suddenly started to laugh before going silent again as a smaller gentleman stepped forward. He had well-developed muscles but looked in weaker shape than most of the training fighters around him.

'I'm Kurt Eiger. Forgive me; most of these guys have done time inside and they don't take kindly to snooping cops as they would see it. Maybe we can go into the office. It's a bit friendlier in there, DC Stewart. And maybe you can tell me where you were trained as that was a smooth move. Very classy.'

Stewart felt herself almost blush but simply said, 'Lead the way,' and then strutted amongst the other fighters over to the office. Kurt Eiger offered both of them coffee before sitting down behind a desk and pointing at a single chair on the opposite side. Stewart offered it to Macleod but he chose to stand and she took centre stage with Eiger.

'I apologise for the rough handedness of one of the guys here. Some are just people who lost their way but there are some who we keep just about on the right side of things if you understand me. They get a little nervy when you show up and you can't blame them for that. But Samuel won't be trying to take on a female officer again in a hurry. He won't live that one down, love. You might as well have just castrated him.' Eiger laughed but Stewart could tell it was a little forced.

'Mr Eiger, does, or did, Sonny King attend this club?'

'Sonny King,' said Eiger his hand to his chin, 'now that's a name I didn't want to hear again. Yes, Sonny was at this gym for a time. But he's gone to the dark side, so to speak. Left me for that lowlife Stones.'

'Gordon Stones? The man who runs the Rehabilitated Offenders Trust?' Stewart saw Eiger nod. 'Why do you say lowlife?'

'Because he is. He's conning these guys, taking them on a ride and taking them to a bad end. Not just a criminal one either.'

'And he's got Sonny King now. In what way, Mr Eiger? Does he have a contract with him? Did he pinch him from you?'

'What contract? You look like you know the game. Most of these guys will never fight for money or anything that really amounts to money. Most will use this to get rid of frustration and maybe use it to protect themselves if their past comes back at them. But Gordon Stones offers them money, and not in the traditional sense.'

'How do you mean?'

Kurt Eiger stood up and paced behind the desk. 'Look, if I tell you, I need you to keep me well out of it. Do you understand? What I'm about to say could get me into a lot of difficulty.'

'Why do you say that?' asked Stewart.

'Because there's illegal fighting going on and it's not pleasant. You've seen a fight that goes on in the octagon. Well, sometimes people get seriously hurt but there's always someone there to stop it, someone to treat the loser straight away. It's a rough sport but we look after the fighters as best we can. These illegal fights have no one watching out for the boys. There's barely a referee in there. More like an entertainments manager if the fight gets too dull, too much grappling.'

'How do you know this?' asked Macleod suddenly. Stewart turned to see her boss giving a penetrating eye to Kurt Eiger.

'Because I was there when one of mine died. Stupid arse got himself involved and I told him not to. But I went to see if I could protect him, from himself as much as anyone else. But he took a hammering and then when the other guy jumped on him, no one stopped it. My boy was defenceless and by the time I was able to get in the octagon, he was gone. Too many punches to the head.'

'Did you not report this?' asked Stewart.

Kurt Eiger looked at Stewart and gave a laugh. 'I'm still here, am I not? So yes, I didn't report it and if you guys say anything, I'll deny it again. There's powerful people running this game, and I'm not even sure who.'

'Who was your fighter that died?' asked Macleod.

'Davie, Davie Magee. Thought himself invincible while he was barely a decent fighter. But in that game, you can be as good as anything and still lose it. Plenty of fixing of fights and money changing hands. And sometimes those watching, I swear, want to see someone killed.'

'How often are these things happening?' asked Stewart.

'Twice a month roughly. Size depends on what venue they can manage and that. That suspected rave three weeks ago? Well it wasn't; it was a fight card and they had to scarper halfway through because some local complained about noise and your guys turned up thinking they had broken up a rave.'

'Did you know Kieran Magee?' asked Stewart.

'I did. I reckon they came for him in that grotto; it's why I'm not surprised to see you. One of Stones's goons, no doubt.'

'Sonny King?'

'Sonny King was the fighter opposite Davie that night. Maybe he was making sure the brother didn't kick off. But Kieran was not at the fight when Davie died. It was incredibly low key, private. Maybe twenty people there, all pretty big deals as far as I could gather. I'm not sure Kieran knew how his brother died.'

'Did Kieran ever fight?' asked Macleod.

'Once upon a time, for me. But he left the game as far as I know. At least I never saw him again in a ring.'

'Could he have been in this underground fighting?'

'Maybe,' said Eiger. 'I've only been to Davie's fight and one other which was much larger.'

'And you don't want to testify to any of this?'

'Don't even go there,' said Eiger. 'If there's a whiff of this, they'll come for me. I'm only telling you so you get off the backs of the boys in here. They're pretty rough but they are clean, going the right way. I don't want Stones to get any more of them.'

'Don't go anywhere,' said Stewart, 'I may need to talk to you again, but I'll try and be more discreet.'

Macleod stepped forward from the wall he was leaning on and Stewart knew he was about to take charge.

'Mr Eiger, I appreciate your situation, but you have just told me about the death, potentially the murder, of Davie Magee. I cannot let that lie. While I appreciate your reticence to come forward, I would like your help to shut down this illegal sport and bring his killer to justice. To that end, let us investigate and help us out in the quiet where you can.'

Kurt Eiger stared at Macleod. 'Do you really know what you are asking?'

Macleod nodded. 'Very much so, and I also know you want

58

to help. What I need is to know when the next fight is, and then you need to get DC Stewart here access to it.'

Chapter 07

Macleod hung his coat up on his office peg and looked around for his empty coffee cup. It was now just after eleven o'clock and he wanted to speak to Hope about the conversation with Kurt Eiger and the bearing it may have on the case. Kieran Magee had been dead less than a day but already he felt as if they were unravelling things. But the drive back through the driving snow had been cold and he was needing a warm cup of his favourite black liquid.

Sticking his head out of his office door, he saw Ross at his desk. 'Where's McGrath?'

'Down at forensics. I think she's just checking in with Miss Nakamura—not sure there's anything new from that side.'

'How are you going with the statements?'

'Nearly all in, so I'll be here tonight pulling them together and seeing if I can make any headway with what happened. Going to be a long one, sir. I've said to Stewart to get some sleep tonight so I can grab a few hours in the morning when she's back in. Are you heading home?'

'Need to tie up with McGrath, but yes, after that, I'll be off.'

Ross smiled. 'Well, give my best to Jane, sir. Hope she's doing well.'

'Coming along but these things take time. But thank you for asking, Ross.'

And that was Ross, always having everything in his head. Macleod had almost forgotten his partner and would give her a call except she'd probably be asleep by now. Still, a quick catch up with McGrath and he'd be done.

Spying a half empty jug of coffee, Macleod took his cup into the main office and filled it up. His fingertips still felt cold and he simply held the cup for a minute, letting his hands warm up. As he was ready to walk back to his office, a hand waved over at him from one of the desks.

'Sir, I have a Mrs Haskins asking for you.' The uniformed officer was waving a telephone at him, but Macleod pointed to his office. This was a turn up. They had not put any pressure on Dermott Haskins and yet his wife was ringing.

Macleod slid onto his chair and picked up his desk phone. Clicking the flashing light, the call came through.

'Hello,' came a husky voice. 'Is that the lead detective?'

'This is DI Macleod, ma'am; how may I assist you?'

'Inspector, I need to talk to you about my husband, Dermott Haskins.'

'Of course, ma'am. Can I suggest you come down here to the station? If needs be, I can send a car to pick you up.'

'No, Inspector, somewhere discreet. It's a delicate matter and I really don't want it on the record.'

Well, then, thought Macleod, *you really should not be making such an open call to the station. We could be recording anything.* 'What are you suggesting, Mrs Haskins?'

'Can you meet me at the old tourist office on the A9 on the way out of Inverness? It has the forest walks beside it and maybe we should take a walk and discuss some things.'

Macleod thought about the weather he had just come through to get back the office. And now this woman wanted to go for a walk. And somewhere dark. But, given the circumstances of her call, Macleod could not really pass on the request.

'I'll be there in half an hour.'

'You'll have to give me until half past midnight, Inspector. I have someone to get rid of. But he's heading out so I shall see you there.' With that, the call was ended. The woman's husky voice rang in Macleod's head as he tried to fathom what she wanted. But nothing came to him and he picked up his mobile, calling Hope.

'McGrath!'

'Hope, I was going to brief you on the visit to the gym with Stewart, but she'll have to do it. And it's worth hearing. Unfortunately, Mrs Haskins has called and asked to meet me late. If it's okay with you, I'll make my way there and see what she's wanting. I don't think it's a sob story for her husband or his business.'

Hope laughed down the phone. 'Secret midnight moonlight rendezvous, and you're asking permission. What if I say no?'

'I'll accept or maybe you could go but she'll probably see me as an easier play.'

'Darn right she will. I'll not tell Jane.'

'You sound in good fettle, Hope.'

'Well, we're making good progress and the conversation with the DCI went well, so yes, I am in good fettle. Go get me some more good news.'

Macleod smiled and closed the call. By the time he sorted himself, it would not be far off half past and if he were early, he could see if Mrs Haskins were really alone. Part of him thought about taking someone with him but he was experienced enough to look after himself. And maybe she'd play the older man card. It was funny what you could learn of people who were trying to play you.

The weather was atrocious as Macleod drove out of Inverness along the A9 before spinning around at Daviot, so he could pull over at the old tourist office on the west side of the carriageway. The place was deserted, unsurprisingly and Macleod drove his vehicle amongst the trees at the forest walk car park. Once parked, he killed his lights. The snow was continuing to fall, and Macleod could see the traffic moving slowly along the A9 as the white, thick blanket began to increase. If this woman wanted a walk it was going to be a short one.

He watched a car indicate and pull off the A9 into the car park he was waiting in. From the shape and headlights, he guessed it was a Mercedes, but Macleod did not move or indicate anything with his car lights. Instead he watched as the car swept around the car park before stopping some twenty feet away. The interior car light came on and he saw a dark-haired woman carefully wrap her head in a scarf and artfully arrange it. Not a common scarf, it looked like it might be silk and when the door opened, the woman got out in a long, red coat with black boots underneath.

Macleod pressed the button and the electric window wound down. 'Mrs Haskins, I presume?'

'Inspector Macleod. Thank you for coming out to see me at this hour. I won't mess you about if you'll take a walk with me. I have something to tell you of great importance.'

'Forgive me,' answered Macleod tersely, 'but won't the car do? It's a bit wild out there.'

'I'd rather not be seen in the car park, Inspector. You don't know who is watching. And besides, being seen would not be the worst of it. Being overheard could be fatal.'

Macleod felt it was all a little too overdramatic, but he flung his scarf around his neck and placed a hat on his head. Jane had bought it for him and it was wide brimmed like something from a bad Western. He had sworn he would never wear it but tonight, it would keep the snowflakes from driving into his face as well as being a perfect disguise. *The strait-laced Inspector in a hat, and one from the movies—never!*

Mrs Haskins slid her arm around Macleod's, and he was suddenly promenading with her towards the forest walk. As he tried to pull away, she gripped tighter. 'It will look like we're just out for a walk if anyone sees us. Don't fret Inspector; I'm not looking for anything. I'm afraid you're too old for me.'

Macleod was not prone to swearing but the comment almost sparked an unholy reaction. Mrs Haskins was not far from Macleod's age, and while she looked extremely neat and to a large degree quite sassy, she was definitely in her later years like himself.

Steered by Mrs Haskins, the pair turned down a wide woodland path, their feet touching the cold ground but now clear of any falling snow due to the shelter of the overhead trees. Small pools of water had turned to ice and Macleod's feet crunched through the occasional piece but in the main, he simply felt cold. His coat was designed to keep off the rain, a hazard of living in Scotland though less so now he was living on the Black Isle. He swore living in Glasgow gave people pointed heads the rain beat so hard at times. Despite the water-repelling qualities of his coat, he was finding it less useful as a barrier against the cold. If only he had brought the new one Jane had got him.

'Have you ever strayed, Inspector?'

Macleod nearly jumped at the comment before composing himself. 'I feel that kind of comment is inappropriate, Mrs Haskins. Indeed, any discussion of my martial or single status is off limits. I'm here for information.'

'Indeed, Inspector, and I was actually referring to myself. I have strayed, you see. I guess you find that quite shocking.'

'I've been in this game so long, Mrs Haskins, truly little shocks me. Except man's inhumanity to man, that never fails to surprise me.'

'Indeed, Inspector, but you might be shocked to know I was in an affair with a man nearly half my age.'

'Was?'

'Indeed, Inspector. It ended this morning; I believe around ten o'clock or sometime after. That's when Kieran Magee died, did he not?'

Macleod could feel it. It was never going to be simple, was it? He had the wife penned as the jealous type and maybe she knew about Mrs Haskins but why was it always messy. No doubt, Mrs Haskins would want it all kept quiet and if he did not keep it that way, she would deny everything in an interview room.

'Does your husband know, Mrs Haskins?'

'No, Inspector, he does not.' There was a pause which caused Macleod to look up at the woman who seemed to be biting her lip, apparently chewing over something in her mind. 'Well, he didn't know about Kieran.'

'Who did he know about?'

'Carlos, lovely Brazilian man, sold mangoes. James, my one-time chauffeur. Kyle, a rather young butler. Then there was

65

Ernesto—'

'Stop! So, you are quite familiar amongst the younger employees or social contacts of your family.'

Mrs Haskins smiled. 'Only the good-looking ones, dear. I'm no trollop.'

'And you considered Mr Magee to be one of the good-looking ones?'

'Well, of course. Kieran worked out a lot and I had the pleasure of watching him train at times. Bit of a bad boy too. I'm afraid I have a bit of a weakness for the bad eggs, as long as they are nice and hot, of course. You really must think the worst of me, Inspector, but I'm just a woman with too much time on her hands and too many formidable bodies coming my way. Well, all except for Dermott, of course. I married him for the money.'

'Did Kieran's wife know you were seeing him?'

Mrs Haskins's sniffed. 'That woman. God, she couldn't handle a real man if he appeared in a pair of tight boxers with a dozen roses. She clearly was not giving Kieran what he needed. I mean I did offer him my time, but he was the one who jumped at it. She was rather clingy from what I gather. Caught up by love, Inspector. Can you imagine, like it's a real thing and not just something the poets keep their job with by pretending it's always afoot. Dear me. Oh, Inspector, I have hurt your feelings.'

Macleod checked his look. Clearly, he had reacted to the idea that love was a made-up nonsense, and that surprised him, for he always kept a straight face. It was Jane's fault. He hoped the thought of her was not currently bringing a ridiculous smile to his face.

'My feelings are not up for debate, Mrs Haskins. Am I correct in assuming that you have come here so that you can tell me this information in confidence? You do realise that my first request is that you accompany me to the station where we can make a formal statement, seeing as you are telling me you had an affair with a murdered man. This puts questions against you, your husband, and also Mrs Magee, never mind any of your previous lovers who may still be infatuated with you.'

'My God, Inspector, you're right. They may still be in love with me. Do you think they could have done it? I mean Dermott wouldn't; Kieran's too valuable to him. But that wife of his. Too strong a love? Or maybe Carlos? Beautiful mangoes but yes, he always seemed like the jealous kind.'

Macleod stopped walking, causing Mrs Haskins to whip around on his arm and then stand before him. The woman was surprised, almost shocked, and he wondered if she was actually delusional. Her manner was larger than life, almost comic book but he could see no hint that this was a set-up. Every fibre of his being told him that Mrs Haskins was really this way and that there was no bluff in her.

'Did you know Davie Magee, Mrs Haskins?'

'Really, Inspector, do you take me for a woman playing two brothers at the same time?'

Every bit of Macleod wanted to scream yes, yes, I do, and it's not a surprise. But instead he remained calm. 'I meant it in the platonic sense, ma'am. I wasn't suggesting anything.'

'Good, because I was only involved with Davie until he died. I became involved with Kieran a good two weeks after that tragedy.'

It took all his years of experience for Macleod not to burst out laughing. And the main reason he did not was that the woman had stated she was involved with a second man who had also died.

'How did Davie die?'

'Business, that's all I know. Dermott mentioned it one night that Davie would not be doing any more work for him, which obviously would have curtailed our rather enjoyable liaisons. When I enquired as to what had happened to him, in case my cover was blown, he simply said business.'

'Do you ever attend any illegal fights?'

'I'm not some sort of riff-raff, Inspector. I only attend quality functions. I don't need to be in the cheap seats. The common thoroughbreds come to me.'

Macleod did not want to point out her rather jumbled-up metaphor and instead took the woman's arm, walking her back to the cars. When he reached the car park, he stood before Mrs Haskins and stared at her from beneath his hat. Some snow had fallen onto it and there was a drip off the brim which fell right before his eyes. Having gone for cool, he hoped it had been a near miss.

'You have opened up a can of worms, Mrs Haskins, and I will probably need to bring you in for interview. If I do, I won't hold back in getting this information from you and onto a recording. You seem to be somewhat flippant about what has occurred. A man has been murdered, Mrs Haskins.'

'Please, call me, Eleanor.'

Macleod was taken off guard. How was that ever a good time to start getting onto first name terms? Watching her face closely, he could see no deception; instead, he saw a woman who had once looked at him with almost disappointment, and who now had a keenness about her visage.

'Do you understand me, Mrs Haskins, or do I need to spell it out?'

'As I said, my dear, it's Eleanor. I do understand you, quite perfectly, but it's bringing out a whole new side to you, Inspector. It's rather refreshing, engaging even. Almost intriguing. What is your first name?'

'Detective! And the second is Inspector. Thank you for the information, Mrs Haskins. I believe we shall be seeing each other in warmer circumstances rather soon.'

'Rather, Inspector.' With that the woman climbed into her car and drove away.

It dawned on Macleod that the woman had thought he was being hard to get, somehow playing a game. Or had she wanted him to see her that way? Whatever she intended, the information she had brought was dynamite. Kylie Magee, no longer a distant partner but a devoted and possibly obsessive wife. Dermott Haskins, a party to Davie Magee's demise. And an affair that could stir up all sorts of bad feelings.

It was now one in the morning and the snow was still falling. Hope would still be in the station and he needed to see her with this information. Tonight was going to be a long one. He thought about ringing Jane to tell her, but she was better asleep. She did not need to know about his snowy, midnight rendezvous. And Hope would take the piss. Maybe that was a good thing for her.

Chapter 08

Macleod entered the station around half past one and found that there was a skeleton staff in the investigation room, but Ross was still at his desk. Before him were a large number of statements, many with fluorescent pen scrawled across them. Making his way over, Macleod was turned away by Ross's wave of his hand and he knew better than to disturb the man. Ross was always polite and if he was shooing Macleod away, it was because his mind was deeply engaged in thoughts he did not want to be removed from.

Macleod poured himself a coffee from the cafetière and sought out Hope. If she were not around the investigation room, then she would be with Jona or else indisposed. The walk to forensics took a good five minutes and Macleod enjoyed the quiet corridors. When he had been in Glasgow, nightshift was a real boon at times. On many occasions, he would get a quiet night and would be able to work away in the calm and not be hassled by his bosses or peers. In many ways, Macleod worked best on his own and he was still remarkably surprised at how well his team had moulded around him.

Once he had opened the door, Macleod realised he had forgotten to knock. He saw Hope rearing back from Jona's

70

shoulder. McGrath wiped her eyes and then sniffed before turning to her superior.

'You're back, sir. Can I help you?'

'We need to have a discussion. Mrs Haskins was quite the character, but she did have some rather revealing information. Maybe my office in ten. I'll leave the two of you in peace. And sorry, I should have knocked.'

'It's fine,' said Jona. 'Maybe I could have a word with you about that cold case you mentioned the other day for me to look into.'

'Sure,' said Macleod, but he had no idea what Jona was on about. Still it was not unknown for him to have spoken and then promptly forget about what he had said.

'I'll see you in ten, sir,' said Hope, leaving.

Once the door was shut, Jona shook her head. 'It frustrates me.'

'That cold case? I'm afraid I can't recall it.'

Jona burst out laughing. The pair had been having regular meditation sessions together and Macleod thought of Jona as a confidant, and a remarkably good counsellor. But he was at a loss to her latest reaction.

'Jona, I really don't understand what is so funny.'

'You are, Seoras. That whole cold case thing was a bluff. I just needed you on your own.' Jona then became more sober. 'She's not doing too well. She said the briefing was one of the hardest things she's done in a long while.'

Macleod thought hard about the team brief he had watched earlier. 'The briefing? She was absolutely fine. Confident, professional. There was nothing wrong in what she did.'

'She said they were all looking, right at her scar. Says that people speak differently to her. Men look away. They don't flirt. Women are different too. Some show real pity which she hates. Others look as if she has failed in the beauty stakes, as if nothing can be done.'

Macleod shook his head. 'I'm not seeing that. People are fairly normal, especially now. I mean at first, the burn on her face did grab you, but then of course it would. But now I don't even think about it. She's still Hope, still attractive, feisty, Hope. Just a bit moodier because she's dwelling on it. I'm trying to let her lead this case to show her how good she is.'

'She said, and frankly, that's not a good move.'

Macleod reared up but then stopped. Jona was better at this sort of thing than he was. The woman had insight, far beyond even what Jane supplied. 'So, what am I doing wrong?'

'You changed. You made a big deal out of it, like she was different and not simply wounded. Suddenly you are watching what she's doing, seeing if she's still got it.'

'That's nonsense, I'm trying to pick her up. Trying to help.

Jona shook her head and pointed a finger in Macleod's chest. 'That's not what she sees. She sees someone who doubts her. All the other stuff, people looking away, men not holding her in their view, well, that's just tough. She needs to know herself and not be so vain about their views. It's always been a flaw in her character. The Allinson thing was bad enough but this she needs to conquer. But then the one person in the world whose opinion of her really matters to her, he starts to show doubts in her. You're a good man, Seoras, even a kind man. But right now, you are also a stupid man. The road to hell is paved with good intentions.'

Macleod stood in silence. Inside he was feeling hollow. Hope was not simply a friend, not a mere colleague. Together they had become a partnership and he realised he had let her down right when she needed him. He was rubbish with how women worked and what they felt but that was no excuse. He had failed her.

'What do I do?'

'Apologise. Explain. Go back to normal. Maybe one day she'll have someone so close all that matters is their opinion, how they see her. However, at this time that person is you.'

'I didn't realise.'

Jona stepped forward and hugged him. 'Of course, you didn't. When you were on your own, you had your God. You still do. Behind it all, what He thinks is what really matters to you. And you are like that to Hope.'

'I'm like her god?'

'Get over yourself, Seoras. You're just a really special friend.'

'I'll sort it. I can put this right.'

'You can,' said Jona, watching Macleod turn for the door. 'Oh, and Inspector.'

'What?'

'You'll make a ham-fisted effort at it, but it'll be enough. And thank you.'

'For what?'

Jona sighed. 'Lately she has not spoken to me like we used to. Your cock-up meant she broke down the walls to speak to me because she was so desperate. Nice work.' Jona smiled and her white teeth shone. Macleod, on the other hand, was unsure how he felt. But it would be put right.

Macleod felt weary as he walked back to his office. It was not the late hour but rather Jona's words. He struggled to understand personal feelings, those deep thoughts of people close to him. Complete strangers or those purveyors of

73

violence he dealt with on a daily basis were no problem. He seemed to get inside the heads of desperate and downright despicable people without trying but anyone close, anyone he actually cared for, seemed to be another world and he did not even have a brochure for the tour.

As he entered the main office, he saw Hope waiting at his door and he fought the urge to tip his head down and shy away from the confrontation he needed to have. Ross was beside her, ridiculously cheery looking for the hour of the morning. Now Ross understood people. No one ever fell out with Ross. Maybe he should give lessons.

'Can you give us a moment, Ross? I'll give you a shout.'

A touch perplexed, Ross nodded and graciously returned to his seat, but Macleod saw he had a worried face when his DC looked back over at this senior colleagues. Macleod ushered Hope into the office.

'I think we are onto something with the Gordon Stones line,' said Hope, a touch nervously.

'Never mind that. I need to apologise to you. I was trying to give you a boost, get yourself back up on your feet because I know you've been struggling lately after the injury. All the words I said to you about how you were still you and that nothing was different, I did mean, but then I undercut you by making you take the lead in the case. I don't have any qualms about your work, Hope. Sorry.'

'Then why do it? I don't understand.'

'Because I saw you take a step backwards and wanted you to run on. I guess I want someone to hand the baton to, and in you, I see that person. That's why I keep muttering about teams and that. It's because I rate you that I did it. But it's my weak point, personal relationships. Let's just get back into the case. Give you a chance to find your own feet, okay?'

Hope grabbed Macleod and hugged him. He stood there, arms out wide not knowing whether he should embrace her or even shoo her off. He was comfortable with Jane's show of emotions, but this was Hope, a figure he struggled with and someone he had managed to keep a professional distance from. But here she was hugging him. Maybe he was broken in his relationships; maybe the woman opposite him was actually more attuned.

'Okay, enough. Go call Ross and let's get after our festive killer.'

When Ross came into Macleod's office, the Inspector noticed that he was staring at the pair of them. The hug must have been evident through the distorted glass. But professional as ever, Ross said nothing. Not even a smirk.

Macleod relayed his encounter with Mrs Haskins to the pair of them and asked for their thoughts. After muttering something about late-night meetings and we should all be so lucky, Hope seemed more serious.

'It seems a bit strange that she looks to cover up her involvement by coming to you. Why not just stay quiet? And then there's the fact she was shag—, intimate with Kieran's brother before he died too. It does make you wonder about Dermott Haskins. Was he capable of performing the strangulation? He didn't look the sort.'

'He must know, surely? She gave off a list of men to you; no husband could be that blind,' said Ross.

'You would think so, but you never know. Or maybe he's actually looking for them. Kieran was quite the figure, especially to Mrs Haskins,' mused Macleod. 'But my money is still on Kylie Magee; after all, it seems she may not be the dispassionate wife she made herself out to be.'

'And on the other side of it all is Gordon Stones; what does he have to do with it? Kurt Eiger was pretty vehement about him. And this illegal fighting where Davie died. Did Dermott set it up or was there something else?' Hope scratched her face, and then stopped as she touched her wound. Her hand flew down from her face and she took on a shocked expression.

'Go on, McGrath, you were in a train of thought.' Macleod smiled as he said the words, believing this show of support was at least not ham-fisted.

'Yes, sorry. I was just . . . the case, I was thinking, maybe we should get someone in on this underground fight ring. Send someone in who knows the score.'

'Stewart?' asked Ross. 'Sounds good; she certainly knows her fighting sports, and she can handle herself better than any of us.'

'I had that same thought but easy,' said Macleod. 'She is still working her way through that attack in Newcastle. I'm not sure she should be in the front line in that way.'

'She operated with Smythe all right in Glasgow, sir,' suggested Hope.

'Okay, I'll talk to her in the morning. How are we suggesting she plays it?'

Hope turned away for a moment, clearly deep in thought before she swung back around. 'I've got it. She goes as a prospective fighter with Kurt Eiger. He can find out the when and where and introduce her so she can get close to the action, get the real lie of the land and who is running this thing. She can see if Kieran Magee was involved and maybe killed because of it.'

'There were a few fighters there,' said Ross. 'You already

know that Gordon Stones and Sonny King were there, but I've also identified an Angus Fischer who strangely enough has a gym membership to Eiger's gym. From my movement chart garnered from the statements taken from everyone there, I cannot rule out any of these fighters from being in the tent. They are all potential killers in terms of where they were.'

'If Fischer is at the gym, then that might be Stewart's best bet to get a low key but informative chat.' Macleod stroked his chin and mused, 'I don't think it's the right connection but we have been informed about a second death that we need to investigate, so we'll run this line of enquiry as well as keeping on at Kylie Magee. McGrath, oversee Stewart's role and see what the pair of you can dig up about Davie Magee's death. How much of an accident was it? And did Kieran truly know? Stones comes under that remit too. Get him rattled along with Sonny King; see where they sit in all of this.

'Ross and I will cover off Haskins and Kylie Magee. I think this is a domestic killing, a jealous lover or an irate wife or husband. Which is fine, I don't mind solving this quickly before Christmas. Oh, and Ross, get into your witness statements and those you cannot eliminate from their location that day, get digging on who they are and if you find any link to our current motley crew, flag it up.'

'Sounds like a plan,' said Hope and yawned. 'Why don't you get off home for a few hours?'

'And wake up Jane—only to leave four hours later. No, I'll just stay here. Keep Ross company.'

It was an hour later when Ross looked up from his computer screen and saw the light go out in Macleod's office. Hope had left for home and now the snores of the Inspector were just about audible. The only other constable in the room looked

77

over at Ross and smiled. *Keep me company,* thought Ross, *as if!*

Chapter 09

Macleod sat in the station canteen, looming over a coffee mug like he was terrorising it. In reality, he was simply letting the aroma waft up his nostrils in an attempt to stay awake. There were four women currently on his mind and surely that was too many. One was Jane, his partner, who was slowly recovering from a previous murder attempt. She was making good progress, especially after a bus crash had previously incapacitated her, but he was worried she was not getting enough support from him now he was back at work.

The second woman was Hope. Things seemed better since the previous night but part of him was concerned about how she needed his faith in her, his trust. She needed to stand alone. Was that not how the new breed of woman was meant to be? Feminism confused him, or maybe it was just women. Either way he struggled, often offending when he truly meant no harm. No, it seemed being on their side was not enough. One had to tread with gentle supportive steps lest you misunderstand the very relationship you were in.

The last two women were much simpler to understand. Macleod was sure Kylie Magee was a killer. His instincts told him so even if he had no proof. She was not at the garden centre. He was on trust with Jona that a skilled, yet weak, attacker could kill by strangulation. But there was something that made him know. He did not buy the aloof wife visage. Eleanor Haskins had decried it too. But then could he really trust her?

Eleanor was aloof herself, detached from the real world, it seemed, but was she ever really lying? One would think a woman coming in this fashion to a police officer was desperately trying to hide something. And yet something in him said she was not. She was simply a creature of that nature who thought the world might work differently. Not that he applauded her stance, jumping into bed with any man who was not her husband. But there was something wondrous in her approach to life.

'Are you going to worship that coffee all day or are you coming to the interview room?'

Macleod looked up at Hope smiling back, albeit a little unsurely. She wore her leather jacket and jeans, which was always a good sign in Macleod's book. 'Neither. Take Ross in with you.'

Hope seemed unsure. 'I thought we were going back to normal.'

'We are and this is. I'm off to Gordon Stone's gym while he's in here making his statement. I want to see what his rehabilitated offenders think of him. It might need a bit of Glasgow hardball.' Macleod lifted his shoulders like he was ready for the fight.

Hope laughed at the gesture. 'Just stick to being you, Seoras; it's frightening enough.'

But her mood seemed lifted. His explanation, and it was genuine, had been accepted and she knew her task this morning. In reality, Stewart should be in there with Hope but Macleod had intercepted the shorter detective and asked her to remain clear of the public areas. If she were going into the fighting game as a new fighter, it would be better if she were unknown. He thought a little make up wouldn't go amiss anyway.

Hauling himself from his seat, his muscles not having yet forgiven him for the lack of a decent sleep, Macleod found his coat in the office before making his way to the car. On his route, he picked up a uniformed officer. Her name was PC Karen Patterson and she was average in height with short brown hair. Nothing about her said she was capable of handling trouble. She might be able to, Macleod really did not know, but the impression he wanted to give the gym was that he was capable of handling trouble. As PC Patterson drove through the snowy Inverness streets, Macleod thought about how to enter. He had two names of potential fighters that might be there. Angus Fischer and Sonny King. Sonny would surely be there, awaiting his boss. They had seemed close before, even if it was a brains and brawn relationship.

Arriving at the Rehabilitated Offenders Trust, Macleod observed it was a reasonably large building with some administrative offices as well as gym and other facilities in the rear. It was not some sloppy outfit Stones was running but Macleod did not trust the outward appearance of anything. Indicating that PC Patterson should come with him, he crunched his way across the white-layered car park and found a receptionist at the entrance hall.

'Hello, I'm DI Macleod and with me is PC Patterson. I wish to talk to one of your previous offenders, an Angus Fischer, ma'am.'

81

The young girl on the reception desk, and she was a girl to Macleod as she looked to be late teens, placed a call to somewhere but then smiled broadly before announcing that Mr Fischer was not on the premises.

'Okay then, how about Sonny King?'

The girl repeated the action without a murmur of displeasure and then advised that Sonny was in the training facility through the large double doors on the left. Giving his thanks, Macleod strode off to the doors and pushed them both back. Inside he saw various mats and gym equipment around a central ring. Not overly busy, there was still a general buzz about the place and Macleod quickly spotted Sonny King in the ring grappling with another man. Dressed in trunks only, King's muscular physique made Macleod promise himself that he would never get to blows with this man.

'Sonny King, I want a word!' barked Macleod over the noise of the gym. Everything went quiet and King broke off from his training bout and walked over to the edge of the ring.

'Mr Stones is with you at the moment. Are you not meant to be with him? He's down the station.'

The incomprehension was written all over the man's face. 'No, Mr King, he's with some of my colleagues but thought I would come and see you. After all, you're the one with all the information, is that not right?' King's face fell and Macleod saw him looking at the exits in the room. 'Just a word, Sonny, that's all. Why not come down and we'll take a wee seat in the corner here?'

'You can't do this?'

'Do what, Sonny?'

'Come in here and demand things of me.'

'Demand, Sonny, who's demanding? I merely come here for

82

a wee word, hoping not to have to bring the rest of these fine gentleman down to the station with me and interview them to find out the things I don't know about you. And maybe find out something I don't know about them. Maybe they don't want me to know those things. But, hey, Sonny, I can go.'

As Macleod turned, he heard the man leap down from the ring and run after him. He might have great physical prowess, but the man was not clever. Macleod had not even begun to play hardball and Sonny had folded. *One should be thankful for small mercies*, thought Macleod.

Sonny took Macleod to a gym locker room and made sure the place was clear before he asked the Inspector and the police constable to sit down on one of the wooden benches between the lockers.

'Don't bring the other lads into it. Mr Stones would not be happy about that.'

'Why, Sonny?' asked Macleod.

'Doesn't like any trouble.'

'But you are all rehabilitated offenders, are you not? What trouble could there be?' Sonny lowered his head. 'How well did you know Kieran Magee, Sonny?'

'Knew him from about. He was into the fighting like me. But he was not as good. Neither he nor his brother were as good as me.'

'Who's his brother?' The question almost floored Sonny as he realised there was an avenue opening up that he did not want to go down.

'Was called Davie?'

'Was called? Did he change it?' asked Macleod.

'No. He's dead.'

'Dead, you don't say. How did that happen, Sonny?'

83

Sonny went quiet for a moment and Macleod could see the cogs turning inside Sonny's head. Macleod was of the belief that there would not be many cogs on the go, but he sat patiently waiting for them to click together.

'Was found at a roadside. Drugs, I think.'

'Drugs, a fighter using drugs; well, I never.'

'Yes, he was a big user.'

Macleod could see the story about to unfold and it was a blatantly false one. He jumped on his man. 'Nonsense, don't lie to me. I can see when you're lying. What happened to Davie Magee?'

'Was left at a roadside like I told you.'

Macleod stood up, his open coat flapping and he took up a rather dramatic pose across from Sonny King. 'Next time you lie, I'm going out there to interview every one of those delightful gentlemen. Understand that.' Macleod paused for a moment for effect. 'Now, what was your relationship to the Magees?'

'I was banging his wife, okay? Nothing funny about it—just getting it on with her.'

'How often?'

'When she called. Usually once to twice a week. Well, at first anyway but then it increased. More like three.'

Macleod was going to ask Sonny if he felt this was sex from a disgruntled housewife, almost trying to get back at her husband but he wondered if Sonny could grasp the concept. 'Was there anything unusual about it?'

'How do you mean?'

'Anything particular to sex with Kylie Magee, something you didn't say or do with anyone else.'

'Well, she called me Tiger, which was fine, but she wanted

to be called Snow Vixen. It was a bit strange but whenever I called her 'babe' she would hit me, sometimes bend my arm in a lock. She could grapple well; she liked that.'

'How well?'

'She pinned me a few times, but she liked me pinning her.'

'She ever ask you to do anything for her, Sonny?'

'Such as?'

'Kill her husband.' Macleod's tone was severe, and he saw Sonny gulp.

'Look, you can nail me to the wall for sleeping with her but that was it. In and out and off home. We didn't have any talks or share anything close. It was just sex. Good sex. I mean I'm good with the ladies.'

I've just accused him of possibly killing another man and he's more concerned about how I perceive he was with the ladies. The man's unreal, or terribly slow.

'So back to Davie; do you really want to tell me what happened?'

'I don't know, I really don't. He was found at the roadside after a fight he was in but that's all I know.'

'What fight?'

'I don't know; I wasn't there.' The throat swallowed and the eyes flickered, and Macleod knew the man was lying.

'So why did he die?'

'Davie was trouble, always trouble. Mr Stones said so.' And then Sonny went quiet. Realising he had dropped his boss in it, Sonny stood up and Macleod watched him walk back to the gym hall. 'If you want anymore, copper, I won't speak until Mr Stones is back, okay?'

Macleod held his hand up to PC Patterson who was about to follow Sonny. 'Let him go, officer. I think he's going to be more useful in the wild than sat in front of me if we play it right. Before we go, let's take a few names and numbers just so Sonny King thinks we are on to something. He does seem the nervous type after all.'

For the next half hour, Macleod stood in the gym hall with his eyes on Sonny King as he wrestled inside the ring. Macleod believed the man would stay there until Macleod left, and he was certainly taking it out on his opponent. Sonny could clearly have strangled Kieran Magee, but Macleod could not see the reason. He would also have to get close and did not seem like the stealthy type.

After a while, Macleod's mobile vibrated and he looked at it, finding a message from Hope. Mr Stones had finished his interview. It was time to go but Macleod made sure he caught Sonny's eye several times on the way out. Well, at least his next stop with Kylie Magee had become a lot more interesting.

Chapter 10

Macleod was feeling buoyed by his success at the gym with Sonny King, and this was needed because his body was not in a celebratory mood. His days of happily managing to stay awake through the night and then racing into the following day were gone. Now he had to drag his body with him, all the while shouting at his mind to take the lead. Age was cruel, and you did not realise it until you got there.

Calling at Kylie Magee's house, Macleod discovered she was out and asked her neighbour where she might be. It seemed that today was a gym day and the dispassionate widow had been seen heading that way already.

The gym in question was the local sports centre and Macleod was again accompanied by PC Patterson as they made their way to the reception desk before being shown the gym. The place looked vast to Macleod, laden with machines of all sorts, as well as a large collection of weights.

It was not difficult to identify Kylie Magee who was on a cross trainer, her arms pumping the upright posts back and forward as her feet moved the pedals beneath in a cyclic motion. Patterson went to attract the woman's attention, but Macleod stopped her with a hand and simply stared at

Kylie. Some people would think the man was enjoying himself looking at this woman's figure, but Macleod was having a more detailed scan. His eyes ran from her hair to her broad shoulders and then along muscular arms to wrists that made his own look fragile. Before, at Kylie's house, she had been covered by baggy clothes and he had not been able to see her contours or muscular definition. Now he did, and Macleod was intrigued.

Macleod's experience of women in fitness clothing was reasonably limited but he had seen two distinct forms in the recent past. Hope was certainly alluring in her sportswear but while she cut a figure it was toned, not overtly muscular. Stewart, on the other hand, had well-defined muscles. She did not look like a body builder, but you could see where her training had paid off. Kylie Magee was more like Stewart and Macleod reckoned she could out bench-press him any day. Although, these days that was not saying much.

Kylie's thighs were also wide, like they had seen many hours of pushing weights. The Lycra shorts were not a fashion item meant to grip and show off her figure; rather, they were an active part of her, keeping those thigh muscles tight and in check.

Macleod strolled up beside the cross trainer and set his hand on the emergency stop button. 'I'd like a word, Mrs Magee, but I do realise you are in full flight so maybe you could join me in a minute. Can I get you a bottle of water?'

'I'm quite busy, Inspector. Maybe you could come back another time,' puffed Kylie.

'As am I and I'm working a murder investigation, so I'm afraid you've been trumped. Far corner, now!' With that Macleod pressed the emergency stop button and the machine stopped. It was less dramatic than a slow down on the treadmill but as the power went out and all the lights on the machine's dashboard died, it was clear to everyone else in the gym that someone was not happy. That person was Macleod, and he had a scowl on his face that made his accompanying PC hold her tongue about not upsetting potential suspects.

'What gives you the right to interrupt my working out? What is so bloody important, Inspector? I told you Kieran and I had drifted apart, and he meant extraordinarily little to me now. I'm not involved.'

Macleod took a bottle of water sitting beside him and opened the cap before slowly drinking about half of the contents and then reclosing the bottle. With the back of his hand, he wiped his mouth dry and then stared at Kylie Magee. 'I will give you this one chance to come clean because you may have had a sensible reason not to tell the truth before. But if you don't tell me now, I will consider you as hostile to our investigations and bring you in for questioning at an appropriate juncture. Now tell me about your relationship with Kieran Magee, your husband,' Macleod emphasised the word, 'and anyone else that caused any friction.'

'I've told you everything, now kindly leave me in peace, Inspector. Although I was no longer in love with Kieran, having your housemate die is still a shock and I'd like to be left alone.'

Macleod watched the scowl on the woman's face and grinned internally. *She thinks I'm here to simply scare her. What would Hope say? Were you banging Sonny King? Let's be a little more refined.*

'Mrs Magee,' started Macleod, 'it has come to my attention that you may have been having intercourse with one Sonny

89

King, who I believe was also known to your husband. I also believe you had him call you by a pet name, which I am guessing is what Kieran used to call you and stopped doing so. Did Kieran stop all relations, Mrs Magee? Was that what the problem was?'

The woman's face fell for a moment but then she recovered and sat down beside Macleod on a plastic stool. She brushed her hair aside and Macleod watched beads of sweat fall from her face, down her neck.

'Have you ever been cheated on, Inspector?' asked Kylie.

'No ma'am, but I have seen plenty of tales where the scorned carry out a wicked vengeance. Did you feel scorned, Kylie? Was it too much to take?'

Kylie lifted her hand to the nape of her neck and ran her fingers up and down. Macleod thought she was trying to put him off guard, almost flirt. If she was looking to bring out his softer side, she did not know him well.

'I will admit that I felt a kick in the teeth, especially as Kieran never admitted to it. He knew about Sonny as well, for I made sure he did. But he didn't care. I was only using Sonny King as a way to get Kieran's attention because they never got on well.'

'And why was that?'

'It was the at the Rehabilitated Offenders Trust that they fell out. At least that's when Kieran mentioned Sonny's name. I have no idea what it was about, but it was serious. Kieran would curse the man's name so when he did the dirty on me, I felt it only fair to give him a proper slap back. But Kieran didn't care.'

'And that gives you a real good reason to kill Kieran, Mrs Magee.'

The woman shook her head and tears began to flow from

her eyes. 'I loved Kieran. Why on earth would I kill him?'

'Some of the strongest lovers have been the worst killers. Maybe you simply didn't want anyone else to have him. Maybe the scorn was too much.'

'Maybe it was, Inspector, and maybe part of me would want to keep him for myself. God knows I have had some dark thoughts these last few days but why in hell's name do you think it was me? I was in the house. I was never at the garden centre. Never had I seen the inside of that damn Santa house where they found him. I was not there.'

And she had handed Macleod the biggest stumbling block to his instincts. She was not there. No one had identified Kylie at the garden centre. Ross had been going through all of the reports and no one mentioned someone looking like Kylie. Macleod kept a straight face but he knew he was beaten for now. With it, his shoulders suddenly became sore and the lack of sleep from the previous night threatened to make everything start to swim before his eyes.

'You'd do better to look at Sonny King, Inspector. I know he wanted a lot more from me. I think he thought he would fill Kieran's place but he's just a puppy on a lead. Not a real man. But he was angry. He knew I still wanted Kieran. Maybe that drove him over the edge. I take it he was there at the garden centre.'

And the weight lifted from Macleod's shoulders. Kylie had gone too far. It was one thing to have asked if Sonny had been at the garden centre, but the way she said it was like she already knew, with the questioning style only there to keep her cover. Had she been there? How? She was on no CCTV. Macleod would need to sit with Ross and go through the camera positions again. As Kylie sat before him, Macleod could see how she could have performed a strangulation of Kieran Magee, but also saw that she was definitely fit enough to make an entrance to avoid any cameras if it were warranted. He just needed to find out the how, and then show she was there.

'I'll take my leave, Mrs Magee; you have been most enlightening. I suggest that next time you start with the truth as not brandishing it makes you look like a liar and that's a hard image to shake.' He hoped it was enough of a barb to make her worry.

Taking his bottle of water, Macleod made his exit from the gym and strode with PC Patterson back to the car. The uniformed officer seemed quite shy and Macleod did worry he might have too fearsome a reputation which caused his colleague not to share. Macleod encouraged sharing, at least in words and on paper. Whether his general demeanour and candour supported these intentions was certainly up for debate.

As he opened the car door, Macleod heard a voice calling after him. Turning, he saw Kylie Magee running across the car park, still dressed in her Lycra shorts and jogging top. He nodded at PC Patterson to get into the car and he swung himself in as well. There was no way he was going to stand and have a conversation out here. It was too cold.

Kylie Magee continued her run across the car park and rapped Macleod's window. Slowly, he reached across for the electronic button that would slide the window down and carefully pressed it.

'Inspector,' said Kylie, a little out of breath, 'I think there's something else you may have missed with regards to Sonny King.'

'I'm listening, but don't mess me about.'

'Davie, Kieran's brother. I think Sonny was involved with his death.'

Macleod narrowed his eyes. 'Apart from being a wild accusation, can you explain further? Was Davie Magee not simply found dead in a ditch?'

The woman nodded her head profusely. 'And who put him there? I believe Sonny King did it.'

'Really. Why?'

'What, Inspector?'

'I asked why. What makes you think that Sonny King killed your brother-in-law?'

The woman looked at Macleod as if he had two heads. 'It's obvious. They hated each other.'

'So, Sonny killed Kieran's brother?'

'Yes!'

'How? And when? And with whom? This is just a wild accusation. Sorry, Mrs Magee, I need to go but if you have anything more substantial to bring to the table then by all means, give me a call. Here's my card.'

Macleod watched the woman take his details in silence. With a delicate finger he activated the window and watched Kylie Magee shake in the cold but fume in her head. From a point of someone hiding behind a detached barrier, he had brought her to the point of scrabbling to maintain a defence. She was guilty as anything but he needed the proof. Until then, he would keep Kylie on tenter hooks wondering if Macleod knew any more. As PC Patterson drove the car away, Macleod pulled down the sun visor and used the vanity mirror to look out of the rear-view mirror. Kylie was still there, and still fuming at Macleod's reluctance to engage her purported theories.

'Sir,' said Patterson, 'do you mind if I say something?'

'I won't know until you have said it, officer.'

'They're right about you. You are one right bastard!'

'If you mean I'm alert and cunning, I'll take the compliment, Constable, but sort out your language. Did they not tell you to speak properly to a senior officer?'

'Yes, sir.'

Chapter 11

Hope had spent the morning bringing Stewart up to speed with the undercover plan they were working out for her. At first, she thought her junior colleague looked rather unsure but when it had been explained that she was going to pretend to be a hungry fighter, Stewart's eyes had lit up. Maybe it was the glory of the Octagon, but something in Stewart had been kindled.

After sending Stewart away to put on a more appropriate form of clothing, Hope made a call to Kurt Eiger at his gym. The trainer was more than a little distressed to hear from her, but Hope explained what she was intending, and the man at least agreed to hear her out on a one-to-one basis.

Aware that Stewart had visited in a professional capacity, Hope set about changing Stewart's look and insisted the glasses went in preference for the contacts that Stewart hated in daily life. She wore them for fighting and without the glasses, Stewart seemed a far less serious character. Hope also sent Stewart to get her hair dyed. When Stewart came back with purple hair, Hope recognised the colour as that of Stewart's favourite cosplay character.

With the fun of the morning out of the way, Stewart seemed to become grimmer as the pair set out for the gym. Maybe she was just getting into character but to Hope, Stewart seemed a little nervous. But her partner looked like a real fighter. Whether she could actually be one if called on, Hope doubted. After all, Stewart did not spend any more time in the gym than Hope did.

Kurt Eiger met the pair as soon as they entered the gym. The atmosphere was workmanlike, and Hope thought it seemed busy. Taking them to a side office, Eiger complimented Hope on the scar on her face.

'Very convincing. Looks like you used to be in the ring yourself. Not that you have the muscle density, but I reckon you would last the distance. You'd just get pummelled if they reached you.'

Unsure if this was a compliment, Hope said, 'It's not me that has to. Kirsten here is your girl.'

'Well, she has the build for it. But if we get called out at this fight we're going to, she has to be able to put up a good show. I'm not walking in there and getting seen for bringing in a daisy. They'll know something is up. Forgive me, love,' he said turning to Stewart, 'but do you mind taking it out to the ring. I want to see you in action.'

'Is that truly necessary?' asked Hope, fearful for Stewart.

'Hope, it's okay,' said Stewart. 'Big sisters, Mr Eiger, always trying to look after you.'

Eiger laughed at Stewart playing her character and strode over to the door of his office. 'Jimmy,' he shouted to someone outside. 'Callen in today?'

'Yes, coach, he's at the back.'

'Tell him I want him ready in the ring in five minutes. He needs to teach some upstart a lesson.'

Hope felt the lump in her throat as Eiger spoke, but Stewart seemed unperturbed. As Eiger left the room, Hope came around behind Stewart and rubbed her shoulders with both hands. 'You okay with this? You don't have to go through with it. You can quit anytime.'

Stewart laughed at Hope. 'You've never been to an MMA club, have you? You don't walk, you bring what you have. If he beats me, then he beats me and I walk away respect intact because I gave it a go. I call it off before I start, and I might as well not look in the mirror.'

Hope watched Stewart strip down to a pair of trunks and a tight fighting top. The woman was so small to be doing this, but Hope admired her spirit. Within a minute, Eiger was sticking his head through the door calling them out to the main gym and to the Octagon in the middle.

The rest of the gym seemed to have downed tools to watch the contest and Hope saw many wondering looks at Stewart as they approached the Octagon. Hope stood to one side as Eiger led Stewart inside, before turning to call for Callen.

The man was at least six feet two and maybe larger. His body in modern parlance was ripped and Hope just saw muscle after muscle. She watched how Stewart never took her eyes off the man but also showed a grimace. Taking a gum shield Stewart shoved it into her mouth and approached the middle of the Octagon for instructions from Eiger. Moments later, Callen and Stewart broke apart, ready to fight.

As Callen strode towards Stewart, Hope saw her colleague skip on her feet. Callen was larger but Stewart seemed to be more fleet of foot. Punches were thrown and Hope saw Stewart rock before a wicked jab caught her on the chin. She stumbled backwards and fell to the ground. Callen dove down after her, but Stewart managed to roll to one side and come away cleanly. But her steps were not so fresh and lively now. That blow must have hurt her.

Hope watched Callen hunt Stewart down from the middle of the ring. Kirsten would back off and just get clear, but the attacks were getting closer. And then it seemed Callen swung with a right hand and caught Stewart's chin. Except she had her hands now on the fist, holding the arm clear as she turned around delivering a whipped foot to the head of the man.

There was silence as the man collapsed to the deck and then simply lay there. 'Next time, bring me a fighter,' said Stewart and simply walked off back to the office. The place went into uproar and Hope watched Stewart being flanked back to the office before she shut the door on everyone.'

'Bloody devious,' said Eiger coming up beside Hope. 'Sold him down the river. She never felt anything he threw; not like she was showing. Your girl's clever, I'll give her that.'

'Then, are we on?'

'In the office; we'll need to iron a few things out.'

Eiger sat down in a low seat and stared at Stewart. 'You can probably pull off the new fighter thing, but there's a lot more at stake here. You can't be too grabby and ask questions here and there. You need to be quiet, observe, not get anyone's backs up. If they suspect anything, they won't hesitate to close us down permanently. I mean they'll come for us like they did Davie.'

'But you said Davie was injured in a fight that simply went too far.'

'And why do you think they let it go that far? These fights, at least the private ones, are less a sport and more like a gladiatorial thing. It's the Romans baying for blood to please the crowd. That's why they are exclusive, people paying big money. And that's where they are making money. Dermott Haskins is involved, I reckon, but I doubt you'll see him there. He's not stupid. You might see Gordon Stones, if one of his boys is fighting. Mainly it will be backroom people, and they change them. And there's a special guy who's there. Like the MC, always in a large mask and a cloak. I reckon it might be different people but he's the boss. And no one knows who he is.'

Hope thought for a moment. 'We could go with a secreted camera?'

'No! Absolutely not,' said Eiger. 'They discover that, we are both dead. Most other things we might be able to talk our way out of. No, we stay simple and you'll see what we see. I'll need a bit of time to organise as well. I haven't been involved recently so I need to make sure I am okay to go before I even ask about your officer.'

'Good,' said Hope, 'but you are on board. This is a starter?'

'Yes, but make sure when you go for it, you do it quickly. I also want a way out if I need to. Catch them in the act rather than any evidence being given in court, if you understand what I mean. I'll lead you to the water, but you have to make the horse drink.'

Hope was not sure the analogy truly worked but she got the gist. The man wanted no part beyond showing them it was happening. Maybe he would feel different once the senior parties were in custody, maybe not. But for now, she had a plan to get Stewart in and she would need to wait for the evening in question, whenever the next private fight would be staged.

On leaving the gym, Hope took Stewart along the road and into a small café. After ordering coffee, she sat looking at Stewart, assessing her.

'What's up?' asked Stewart.

'Are you sure you're all right with this, especially after that Newcastle episode. If you get involved in anything and you shut down, you might not come out of this one.'

'It's different. There's a ring, or an octagon, and there's a single opponent. I'll have my fists. Trust me it's different. The girl in Newcastle dropped her boyfriend. It wasn't the violence; it was the way she carried it out. I couldn't stop it. This is about me and no one else. It's different, boss.'

Hope was unsure if it truly was, but she decided not to quibble with Stewart, and they sat in silence drinking. *What was it Macleod had said when she had first got to Sergeant? She needed to bond better with Stewart.*

'How's your brother?'

'Fine,' replied Stewart.

Hope nodded at Stewart and chewed over another mouthful of coffee. 'Tell me, Kirsten, do you really enjoy the fighting? I mean there will be a load of guys chanting and calling. I guess you'll be a bit on show if you make it into a ring when you go. They were certainly all round you when you dropped that Callen guy. Do you enjoy it?'

Stewart seemed to blush. 'I do. Nice to be noticed. I guess you never have that problem.'

'I'm afraid it's going to be a more common problem now than before,' said Hope.

Stewart looked angry and was about to say something when Hope saw she was holding herself back.

'Go on; say what you're thinking.'

Stewart shook her head and then looked up at Hope. Their stares held until Hope opened her hands indicating she wanted Stewart to share. Stewart took in a deep breath.

'Frankly, get over yourself. You have a scar on your face. Big deal. My brother has the mental age of an eight-year-old and struggles to fit into any society, so much so he has a carer making sure he doesn't do something daft. Whereas you have a scar from saving someone's life, which guys are going to dig. And the rest of your body hasn't changed. Try being a five-foot nothing geek with glasses and getting a look. Seriously, Sergeant, what are you so down about?'

Hope was perfectly still, almost in shock. Stewart was still looking at her and if she had been wearing her glasses, Hope was sure they would have been pushed back in anger.

'I'll take a walk and see you back here in ten minutes,' said Stewart, escaping the tension in the air.

Hope placed her elbows on the table and dropped her face into her hands. Was she really that obsessed with herself? She had no one. When Jona had started her meditations with Macleod, Hope had pushed her away. When the scar had happened, she had made it the *thing*. Macleod had been there for her, trying to support in his own dumb way but all she saw was someone who had lost faith in her. And why did she seek his okay?

Hope had never seen herself as self-obsessed but right now she felt like she was totally that character. Part of her even recognised that she was jealous of all the guys at the gym following Stewart back to the little office. It was all a bit too much to process and Hope wondered what she should do. But there was work to cling to, so let's get on with that.

As if on cue, a text message arrived from Kurt Eiger. He had communicated with some of the people who advised him that there was a fight that night and that he would be more than welcome. The actual location would be sent by text later but, yes, he could bring along a new fighter for people to look at.

Sweet, thought Hope, *at least I have something else to talk to Stewart about and not her comments. How do you address them, especially if she is correct? Bugger it.*

Hope saw Stewart coming back into the café and got up, pointing behind Stewart towards the door. 'Time to go get you ready, because we are on tonight.'

Chapter 12

'So, Ross, this Angus Fischer character was there on the CCTV and he's definitely in the MMA crowd?' asked Macleod as the car pulled up to the driveway of a small, detached house on the edge of Inverness. There was a light on above the door and Macleod could see a small garage at the rear with some junk lying around in front of it.

Walking through the snow to the front door, Macleod thought about Stewart going to the illegal fight that night and wondered if Hope would be able to tail her in any way. He had advised caution and to not get close at all, but he knew Hope would try anyway. Stewart had been advised to simply get in and out and report all she had seen. She was not to engage anyone unless she was spoken to.

Ross rapped the large brass knocker on the lime green door and Macleod realised, even with his total ineptitude in the retail furnishings department that most of the items on this house had been randomly placed. There was no style, just function. *Men must live here*, is what Jane would have said. And she would probably be right.

When the door opened, Macleod found himself looking up into the eyes of a blond-haired man whose shoulders seemed to struggle to pass through the opening. His fists were like large palm trees and in Glasgow surely, they would have described them as bats, not hands. But the man's face was friendly enough although he pulled his smile in when Ross flashed his warrant card.

'DC Ross and this is Detective Inspector Macleod. Are we speaking to Angus Fischer?'

'Yes, you are. Is something wrong?' Fischer pushed a hand through his mop of coarse, blond hair.

'I believe you were at the garden centre when the body of a man playing Santa Claus was found,' said Macleod.

'You're talking about Kieran. Yes, I was there.'

'Can I ask what your purpose there was, Mr Fischer?'

'Sure, Inspector. I was seeking out a job from Mr Haskins. I got word from a lot of the lads that Mr Haskins was hiring for the Santa jobs and I thought I would chance my arm. He was busy when I called at first due to the garden centre grotto opening, so I decided I would simply hang about, Inspector, catch him once things were underway.'

Macleod could feel the cold on his shoulders and saw the first flakes of another snowfall beginning to descend. 'Was it not a bit late to start offering yourself for Santa work? I mean, it's December. I'd have thought all the jobs would be taken up.'

'As did I but with money being an issue, I gave it a punt, Inspector. As it was, it worked out because I managed to get him the following morning and I'm going to be Santa up at the shopping centre in town.'

'So, if I understand this correctly, Mr Haskins is organising all these grottos. I mean, are there more than these two?'

'I think there's at least ten, some out in the community halls in the estates and that. There's been a big push behind it.'

Macleod pondered on this. 'If it's been such a big push, then

104

why wasn't the job you're going to filled up? I'd have thought that the supermarket would have been a prime one to have sorted.'

'Well, it was. Kieran had it, along with Johnny Myers. I believe the two of them would be the supermarket and Kieran up here. You see the garden centre was going to be closing at five except for the odd late night and Johnny would have completed all day in the shopping centre. There was room for a third person but Kieran wanted the extra time, so he was going to be taking over from Johnny. In fact, Johnny started today, and I'll be out there as of seven. I'm just grabbing some dinner before I go.'

'Can we come in, Mr Fischer? It's just we have a few more detailed questions about subjects that are not meant for doorstep discussion. We won't keep you long.' As if to emphasis his point, Macleod turned up the collar on his coat and stamped his feet. He looked disapprovingly at Ross who stood upright and without a flinch like he was standing in the sun-soaked Mediterranean.

'Well, I . . .'

'Something wrong, Mr Fischer?'

There was a shuffle of feet behind Macleod and he turned to see a shadow beyond the driveway. 'Did you see something there?' asked Ross to Fischer.

'No, it's nothing, I was just looking at my time. You'd better make it quick.'

As Fischer withdrew, Macleod stepped onto a dark green carpet, the snow falling from his shoes onto the fabric. Following Fischer's indications, he turned left into a small lounge where a fire was burning low. Without asking, Macleod took up the seat nearest the fire and put his hands out to it. The heat was not strong but at least it was something.

'Now, Mr Fischer,' started Macleod as the man entered the room, 'I've been told you are one of these mixed martial arts fighters. Is that correct?'

'It is, Inspector.'

'And do you have a gym you frequent?'

'Yes. Kurt Eiger's my trainer.'

'And you have previous convictions for GBH, I believe.'

'All spent, Inspector. I'm sure my records told you this.'

'They did indeed, Mr Fischer. Are you also a member of the Rehabilitated Offenders Trust?'

'I am but I don't have many dealings with Gordon Stones. He's not very kosher, Inspector.'

Macleod saw the smallest beads of sweat form on the man's brow. 'In what way, Mr Fischer?'

'Nothing I would like to say as I get it all on second-hand reports. We talk to each other, as ex-offenders because you go through a lot of the same things. Sometimes you have to stay clear of some people.'

'That's interesting as I thought Mr Stones was supplying the Santa Claus personnel for these grottos and yet you seem to have secured a job.'

'I believe Mr Haskins has the contract and with Kieran's sad demise I caught him at the right moment. I'm not sure Mr Stones was consulted. I certainly would not have gone through Gordon Stones.' Fischer spat into the fire.

Macleod felt a little frustrated as he hoped Fischer might have broken ranks and given up some detail like Eiger had on the fighting ring, but the man was sombre. But maybe he needed to come at this more directly.

'We've heard reports of underground fighting going on in

the MMA circles, Mr Fischer. You aware of any?'

The man walked over to the door. 'I need to get my coat, Inspector, as I'll be off soon.'

'Apparently, one fighter, Davie Magee, lost his life at a fight.'

Fischer turned abruptly. 'Shush, lower your voice. You don't talk about things like that.'

'Like what?' asked Macleod.

'Davie!' hissed Fischer. 'The people that hold these fights; they don't take risks. They hear anything, find any nose poking its way in and they deal with it. Davie was loud mouthed, too loud mouthed.'

'What do you mean by that?' asked Ross.

'Got a little bit of success, started blabbing to people. Then he strangely dies in his next bout.'

Macleod stood up. 'Are you telling me that it was not a fair fight, that they made sure he would die?'

'All I know is that Davie should have won that fight hands down. He told me he would win, told me who his opponent was, and I agreed. But Davie ends up at the roadside.'

'Who was his opponent?'

'I said Davie ended up on the roadside, or did I not make myself clear? They would kill anyone who interfered. I don't have much, but I have my life.'

Fischer stepped outside the room and grabbed his coat. Macleod followed into the hallway and pointed a finger at Fischer. 'You know who killed Davie Magee, and now someone has killed his brother. That's more than enough for me to pull you down the station. I'm guessing that won't go down too well in your community so I'm suggesting right now that you give me a bit more of the word out there. What's happening here?'

Fischer was visibly sweating, and he almost started to crouch and make himself smaller, as if this would lower his voice. In a whisper he began to speak to Macleod. 'Stones is supplying the guys for these fights. It used to be lots of different gyms, but they stopped that after Davie Magee died. I think Kurt Eiger was warned off. He went with Davie that night, but he told everyone he saw Davie safely home.'

'Could Kurt have killed him,' asked Macleod, his mind on a certain Constable he had sent off with Eiger that night.

'No, Kurt is solid. He's just keeping his head down, scared like we all are.'

'Was Davie dead when Kurt left him?'

'I don't know for sure, but I heard that Kurt tried to stop the fight. He was too late. Rumour is Davie's opponent had a spike in his hand that he punctured Davie's head with. But that might be rumour, as I didn't ask anyone for clarification, if you understand me.'

Macleod placed a hand on Fischer's shoulder. 'Who was Davie's opponent that night?'

'Tell no one. Don't give it away anywhere or they might come for me. Sonny King.'

'Really!'

'You heard me. Now I need to go, or I'll be late and they'll ask why. You weren't here, Inspector; help me out with that if anyone asks.'

Macleod gave a nod to Ross and they made for the front door and stepped back out into the snow. As Fischer closed the door behind him, Macleod stared off into the night. As Ross went to see what he was staring at, Macleod motioned to the car and Ross followed whilst Angus Fischer made his way to the street and walked off in the opposite direction.

Ross drove the car away but as soon as he had left Fischer's street behind him, Macleod indicated that Ross should stop. Pulling over, he looked at his boss inquisitively, before Macleod asked Ross to get out. Together they walked back to Fischer's street and Ross was told to keep an eye out, looking for anyone who might be watching the house.

Macleod made his way back up Fischer's drive but instead of going to the door, he circled the house. As he reached the side of the building, he saw a footprint in the snow and a then a few more. He found further impressions around the rear of the house. Carefully Macleod took a ruler from his pocket and dropped it beside a footprint. With his mobile, he lit up the scene and took an image of the footprint. Looking around, he found more complete prints and took more photos.

Ross was walking along the street as if he were enjoying a bracing stroll, but Macleod thought he looked strange in his shirt and tie under the coat, black polished shoes on his feet. Surely, walking boots would be the more obvious choice. But then neither of them thought they would be involved in a little reconnaissance.

'Anything, Ross?'

'No one I can see, sir. You get anything?'

Macleod nodded. 'Someone was at the house, possibly listening. Get someone down to the shopping centre and make sure Mr Fischer is there. Nothing too close, just observing. We should try and see Mr Stones right now, and possibly Mr Haskins. I want to see if they are at this fight.'

'Yes, sir,' said Ross and turned back around, making his way back to the car. As Macleod followed, he began to get a sinking feeling. Inside, he was sure Kylie Magee had killed her husband; he just had no evidence. But he feared there was more going on and he was about to be launched into the middle of a haystack looking for a tiny murderer. It was a metaphor he fell back to after he dreamed it one night in Glasgow. It was the tiny cuffs in the dream that had genuinely surprised him.

Ross drove Macleod to Gordon Stones's house only to find it in darkness. Taking a spin round to the Rehabilitated Offenders Trust offices, they found them closed. Macleod was not surprised but proving that Gordon Stones went to the illegal fight would be dependent on his young DC.

Driving up to a rather expensive house in the country surrounding Inverness, Macleod marvelled at how much a garden centre could bring in for its owner. The hedges around the house were immaculate and the house itself was like an Edwardian country mansion, or as near to one as Macleod could imagine. He was no architect, and his understanding of period houses was limited, but this was magnificent. There were even pillars either side of the main door. You never saw a lot of that in Glasgow. At least not where Macleod's investigations had taken him.

Crunching through freshly laid snow, Macleod made his way to the large front door and rang the bell. The door remained impassive, but Macleod could hear someone running around behind. After two minutes, the door opened and Eleanor Haskins appeared in her silk dressing gown. The item was not particularly revealing but it was elegantly cut, and she gave off a classy figure. But Macleod nearly laughed at the long cigarette holder in her mouth. The end of the cigarette was not glowing and there was no smell, but Mrs Haskins seemed to act as if she was enjoying the inhalation of the non-existent fumes.

'Good grief, Inspector, and on such a cold night. It's okay

Hughie, you can come out; it's only the Inspector.'

Macleod wondered who Hughie was until a man in boxer shorts appeared. The man had a superb set of abs but seemed to be at least twenty to thirty years younger than Mrs Haskins. Hughie also seemed to be waiting for instruction from Eleanor and he simply hung around in the background while the woman surveyed Macleod.

'I do like a man on the job. I take it you are here looking for my husband. As you can tell from Hughie's presence, Dermott is not about. In fact, he won't be back tonight. Screwing some blonde bit, no doubt. Doesn't appreciate an older woman, Inspector. Not like you do. If you want to come in, I can send Hughie home. He's a good boy, won't tell anyone.'

The woman was a tour de force. Whilst she was not stunning in her figure, she had an allure caused by her actions and tone. Her directness was somehow outrageous but also deeply inviting and Macleod found it hard not to like her despite the crazy pass she had just made at him.

'I'm afraid I'm on duty, ma'am.'

'I know, Inspector, otherwise you would and of course your dedication to duty is one of your best turn-ons but I am disappointed. These young bucks are all about the action with none of the sophistication. Still, I shall make do.'

Macleod found himself grinning at the situation, but he tried to force a serious question out. 'Do you know where your husband is tonight?'

'No, I don't and frankly, I don't care. We are like two passing ships in the night with all canons pointed at each other.'

'What time did he go out?'

Eleanor Haskins threw her hair back in annoyance. 'He never came home from the office, a fact he told me this morning but really, Inspector, can I tempt you into a little fun? Maybe a sherry? No, a serious malt would be you? One from Islay?'

'I don't drink, ma'am.' *What has that got to do with anything?* thought Macleod. 'I'll not trouble you much further, Mrs Haskins, but which car is he in?'

'Eleanor, Inspector, and not another Mrs Haskins from you. He has the Jaguar.' Eleanor rhymed off the number plate like it was her children's names. 'But it'll be at the garden centre. He always gets a taxi or a car from somewhere if he's out late. Who knows what he sticks down his nose and throat at these shindigs? Anyway, as much as I enjoy talking to you, Inspector, and as much as I'd like to be more comfortable discussing whatever excites you, poor Hughie is waning here and I need to make use of what time he has left available. If there's nothing else . . .'

Macleod shook his head and started to chortle as he turned his back on the now-closed door. There was something terribly disarming about the wild woman and whilst he laughed, Macleod knew that made her a dangerous suspect. She was too easy to dismiss. But more importantly, Dermott Haskins and Gordon Stones were not at home. But were they at the fight?

Chapter 13

Stewart almost skipped from her house as she made her way to the bus stop along the road. Her brother had his caregiver with him, and she was set for probably one of her best adventures as a police detective. Her hair was tied back, and she wore a tight beanie on her head. An orange bubble jacket kept her warm along with thick tracksuit bottoms but underneath she was dressed for combat if needed. The tight top and shorts gave excellent mobility as well as stabilising any parts of her that were liable to jump about. In her pockets she had her gloves, and she knew she looked good.

It may be that she would not have to show her abilities in the Octagon, but part of Stewart wanted to. The showdown at the gym had given her a terrific confidence and even the warnings of her boss had not dampened her enthusiasm.

'Get in, survey, get out,' the Sergeant had said, and Stewart certainly was keeping that as her intention. However, if a demonstration were required, she would be happy to oblige. Kurt Eiger had said he would pick her up at the gym, which meant he would not know where Stewart lived, always a sensible precaution. Sergeant McGrath was going to tail them from the gym but there was no guarantee she would be able to stay on the tail undetected. The one thing she would not do would be to give the game away.

Snow was falling heavily and Stewart watched the wind picking up, making the flakes swirl here and there, occasionally lifting them back up as well as down. It was certainly no night to be outside. The bus was crowded and Stewart stood for most of the journey. This was ostensibly to allow an older woman to sit down but really, she was too excited. This would be fine for her cover as an aspiring fighter.

Kurt Eiger was dressed in a large black leather jacket and he watched Stewart from a hatchback in the gym car park. Slipping into the passenger seat, there was only an 'Okay?' from Eiger and Stewart nodded. The journey to their next stop was short and they arrived at an abandoned building site on the edge of Inverness. In the distance, Stewart could hear a flight probably landing at the local airport.

They were sitting in the car for a good half hour before another vehicle arrived. It was a black transit van and Stewart made a note of the number plate in her head. Three men got out, all over six feet and well built, before opening the rear doors and indicating that Stewart and Eiger should get in. Once inside, the men, having checked that neither of them had any phones or ID on them, took blindfolds and began to tie them across the travellers' faces. Stewart gave Eiger a look of worry, but he said out loud that this was normal.

'It's her first time but you should see her fists go.' The men did not seem impressed, but neither were they put out by Stewart's concerned look.

The vehicle started and sitting on her bottom in the rear of it, Stewart found herself swinging about as they went round corners. Trying to picture in her mind where they were, all she could really say was that after ten minutes, she was struggling to hear any other vehicles. At one point they stopped for five minutes before other people were introduced to the rear of the van.

When the vehicle stopped for the last time, it was another ten minutes before the blindfolds were removed. Stewart saw four men and two women beside her other than Eiger.

'These are the other fighters,' whispered Eiger. 'See how the hands are already taped up, ready to fight. I don't think we are going into the expensive seats tonight but on the other hand there are even numbers there, so you probably will not be required to fight.'

Stewart nodded and expressed some slight relief but inside she was actually disappointed. One of the three men who had brought her in the van, offered an open hand and led Eiger and Stewart from the van into a large hall with dim lighting.

'Bit different from last time you were here, Eiger,' said the man. 'Been some difficulties so all the punters wear masks to hide their identity. Of course, we don't get any. There's also a new pit, Eiger, very neat and very cold. The fighters start from here but if you follow me, I'll show you to the cheap seats.'

The man led the pair through a small archway and along a granite corridor. Turning around a corner, they were suddenly confronted with a small balcony with seats. Beyond the balcony was a pit maybe twenty yards wide and elliptical in shape. Their seats were at the thinner portion and afforded a decent view of the pit but above them, Stewart could see some high-quality cushioned seats with masked figures and a number of scantily clad women serving drinks.

Stewart cursed under her breath. There was little to see here, certainly no faces. All she had to tie in to were the three men who had delivered them in the van and the fighters. No one of any importance was identifiable. Yes, she might pick out shapes and numbers of males and females, but she could hardly simply stare at them all without blowing her cover. And there were certainly no risks being taken in the higher seats as masks remained firmly before faces. Even drinks were sipped through a straw to avoid the masks being removed. The masks in question were gold but as to whether they were made from real gold or were even plated, or just painted, Stewart had no idea.

A sound from below made her look into the pit and she saw the two female fighters enter. They seemed to be wearing distinctly less than when they were in the van.

'Is this some sort of porno or can these girls really fight?' asked Stewart.

'It'll be real, and they'll be getting good money if they win,' answered Eiger. 'If you note that most of the watchers above are men, that's why the outfits are so sexualised. If you fight, you'll be wearing one too.'

Stewart felt a little sick at the idea. She was all for showing her prowess in a fight but she hated the idea of being leered at. Her cosplay ideas when she had visited comic book conferences and the scantily clad outfits she had occasionally worn had always seemed fun. Here, without a choice, it all seemed vulgar and sordid.

A figure in black, sporting a cloak and mask, entered the ring and began to wave at the two fighters pushing them back to their corners. He then casually threw a whip on the ground and a baseball bat.

'This is different,' said Eiger. 'Clearly things have moved on because this is more like a Roman Amphitheatre. I don't know how far this is going to go but whatever happens, don't break cover,' he said in a low voice.

Stewart stared in horrified fascination as one woman scrambled for the whip. She was maybe thirty years of age and well-toned, but the woman opposite was much larger. In a normal octagon, this weight match would not have been allowed but this was nothing normal.

The larger woman picked up the baseball bat and began swinging it and running up close to her opponent. But the woman with the whip was canny and simply flicked out with it as the woman approached, striking her each time. Soon there was blood flowing from the larger woman's face, but she still approached. In a moment, Stewart saw the whip miss and the larger woman raced in delivering a blow towards the head which caused the smaller woman to fall. Once she was on the ground, her opponent opened up with blows to the body and the smaller woman covered up. After hitting her some ten times, the larger woman leered close calling out at the smaller woman. Upstairs people shouted, calling for a finish. Despite their being only maybe ten to fifteen people up there, the noise was deafening in the small arena and Stewart felt the blood rush from above.

But as the larger woman bent close to call out her opponent, the smaller woman slipped the whip around the larger woman's neck. Quickly working her way behind the woman, she pulled the whip tight and the larger woman dropped the baseball bat. Stewart saw her choke and then collapse to the ground before the smaller woman began to beat her with the discarded baseball bat. There was blood on the metal floor of the arena which ran with abandon. The larger woman was not getting up. And then the masked man in a cloak jumped into the arena again announcing the winner.

The eyes of the winner looked cold and she bore her own bruises and cuts. The three men who had brought Stewart to the arena were now engaged in dragging the larger woman from the pit. Stewart saw she was breathing but she looked a bloody mess.

The fight had lasted maybe five minutes, but it had clearly delighted those above. Without delay, as soon as the previous fight had been removed from the pit, two male fighters came in, dressed in trunks and with bare torsos.

Unlike the previous fight, this one had no weapons but for that, it was no less brutal. Stewart watched as each fighter battered chunks out of the other until one gained a decisive upper hand and simply grabbed the head of the other whilst pinning him down from above, before repeatedly smashing the face of his opponent into the hard metal floor. Again, Stewart was unsure of the status of the loser as he was dragged from the arena.

An underlying horror was building up in Stewart as she realised this was going on, not in some foreign land, but where she lived. But part of her also wondered who was paying to see this, and what money was being made above. In truth she was shocked, and she could tell Eiger was as well. She had been expecting a rough bar brawl fight or a simple illegal punch up, but this had evolved. Someone knew how to market and deliver such a sick show.

Stewart was expecting the final fight to be immediately after the second one had concluded but for some reason there seemed a delay. Those above started to get agitated as neither the fighters nor the man in the black mask and cloak showed their faces. Beside her, Eiger seemed to be agitated.

'Something's wrong,' said Eiger. 'Look above, they are not

used to this delay. I guess they want to get in and then out fairly quickly once the actual fights begin.'

Stewart shook her head. 'I have a different thought. Maybe they get a kill in the last fight. Maybe that's what they want. They seem to have the lust for it.'

As Stewart stood up to supposedly stretch her legs, but in reality, to see if she could garner any further information, she heard footsteps behind her. Turning around, Stewart saw the three men who had brought her there and one was holding a large spear, pointed right at her chest. One of the other men stepped forward and took off her jacket before grabbing her by the neck, shoving her towards the edge of the balcony. Before she could react, she was grabbed by another set of hands and tipped over, dropping the ten feet to the metal arena below. Stewart managed to orientate her feet so they landed first and then collapse her knees, so she rolled onto the cold surface. As she stood, Eiger fell to the ground beside her. He did not fall so smoothly and landed on his side, crying out in pain.

Stewart bent over and helped Eiger to his feet. As they stood up, two fighters stepped into the arena from the normal opening. Stewart recognised them from those who had travelled in the van and she felt her heart pound. These guys could be proper fighters. She was out of her depth. All her bravado as she had left the house was now sinking and she fought to control her thoughts. Behind the fighters, the man in the black cloak and mask stepped into the ring and strode before them as the audience above began to shout.

From beneath his cloak he pulled out a gun and shouted at the two fighters in their trunks to, 'kill them or be killed yourselves.' His finger was pointed at Stewart and Eiger.

Chapter 14

'Go back to back,' Eiger shouted at Stewart. In a whisper he added, 'When I attack mine turn and run past me. Go for the exit and get help.'

'I can't leave you,' Stewart replied in a hushed tone.

'I can't run and there's too many of them. You need to run and find help; otherwise, we're dead.'

Stewart's heart pounded as she saw the two fighters approach. Each was larger than her but at her diminutive height that was nothing unusual. Turning her back to Eiger, she also kept one eye on the man in the black cape and mask who was still holding a gun, watching the proceedings. She could not simply run and hope to escape a bullet. She would have to time her escape when he was not looking and give him a blow on the way past.

The noise from the people watching grew as Stewart and Eiger were encircled by the two fighters. Stewart glanced up and quickly looked at the small balcony where she had been sitting minutes ago. She counted two of the men from the van there. Where was the other one? Her hands began to shake, and she pulled them tight into fists. A terror was growing in her but the dominant tiger that she brought out at the gym several times a week was also stirring in a way she had never known before.

During her time going to her mixed martial arts gym, Stewart had been told she was extremely calculating in her fighting technique. Methodical and usually calm, she would struggle to unleash everything within her. Maybe that was the forced situation of the gym, a fight but a controlled one, and two friends trading blows. Now, as she watched a man looking to kill her come before her, something else was rising. Was it a darkness as she looked at her opponent? Or was it simply her survival instincts woken from their slumber?

Her opponent threw a quick jab and she swayed out of the path of what would have been a decent strike if not one to finish her. A few more jabs followed, and she felt he was trying to weigh her up. Stewart swung a leg making the man keep his distance as she waited for Eiger to begin his plan. There had to be no hesitation on her part; she had to simply execute. Even now, her logical and incisive brain was taking apart the fight and giving options to her depending on how these first few moments went. But at the fore of her mind was the gun held by the man in the cloak.

Behind her, she heard Eiger engage his opponent and then he was tumbling past her in a grapple, pulling his man to the ground and into her own opponent. She saw her attacker drop to his knees, striking out at Eiger who had his opponent in a loose neck choke on the ground. A glance at the man in the cape showed him to be looking up at the audience above, hands outraised as if to say, 'Here's the show'.

Stewart ran straight to the cloaked man while her opponent was engaged with Eiger. The ground to cover was short and he had not even realised she was there by the time she had delivered a punch straight to his chin. Her hand stung but she

121

saw him stumble and fall, causing the gun to slip out of his hand onto the metal floor. It slid away from the pair of them and Stewart for a moment thought about grabbing it, but then she saw the exit. The gun would be a risk and if there was one person armed here there may be more. Eiger had said to flee and he was right. Without looking back, Stewart bolted straight for the open exit.

There had been two of the men from the van on the balcony and she spotted the third as she ran through the archway to the outside bay where the van had been parked. The man was reading a paper, a tabloid and staring at a picture. He looked up as he heard shouts from the arena, but Stewart reached him before he could react and drove his face straight into the bonnet of the van the paper was laid out on. The man fell but Stewart did not stop to see if he would recover and come after her. Instead she saw the door in the far wall.

It was a sliding door that descended from the roof, one found in many garages and Stewart saw the operating panel beside it. Pressing the up button, she found the doors barely moved. She tried again but this time held the button down. The door slid up and as soon as it had reached a foot high, she dove for the ground to roll under. As she did so, she could see someone coming into the room and hoped they would not have the gun. Gunfire reverberated as she heard the door rattle, presumably from a shot that missed above her. Although her heart skipped a beat, Stewart did not stop and rolled out onto a concrete floor that sloped upwards. The air here was cool, and she guessed she was already outside if in a sheltered spot.

Running up the slope, Stewart heard shouts behind her, but it was all frantic. On either side of her was a tall building and she noted it as not quite a castle but more like a Scottish stately home. She could be anywhere. But the first priority was to run until she found cover.

One of the positives that came from her training at the MMA gym was that Stewart was extremely fit. Not simply someone who could unleash a decent kick but in terms of her cardio fitness, she had improved greatly over the last few years and now could last a good three rounds in the Octagon. That was no mean feat when you had to keep on your toes and unleash punches and kicks while all the time keeping a constant focus. Right now, she was thankful for all the time she had spent as she ran as hard as she could up the slope searching for cover.

Reaching the top of the slope, Stewart heard the metal door sliding open. Desperately she looked for somewhere to hide but saw a large lawn before her with what looked like gardens in the dark. There was no moon due to the clouds and snow which would have happily reflected any light was simply a confusing dim blanket. Still, she ran for all she had towards the supposed gardens realising she may be able to get some type of cover.

As she cleared the building, the wind felt stronger as she realised she had been shielded from it. But now in the open, her arms felt the cold, clad in only her fighting top and the track bottoms. If she could make a successful initial escape, Stewart would probably need some form of shelter for the night. She wondered what the time was but ignored her watch, running hard for the garden.

There should have been more of a chase after her, surely. She had heard the garage door go up. Now she had gained ground from the stately home, Stewart glanced back and saw a single figure at the top of the slope. It was the man in the cloak and mask, and he was simply staring out at her some four hundred metres away. *Good,* she thought, *they are disorganised, so I need to put this advantage to use. He'll have his guests to worry about. They'll want me captured quick, but they'll also be wanting to get out quickly, lest I bring anyone back.*

And then Stewart thought about Eiger, his selflessness and sharp mind. He had drawn them in to give her a chance. But he would soon be dead, if not already. Maybe that was what happened to Kieran Magee. Had he been caught up in this? Certainly, his brother had to some degree.

As she reached the garden, Stewart saw shapes loom up in the darkness. As she bolted between the gap between two looming walls, she realised she was in a long channel with plants on either side. Or rather what seemed to remain of plants for the vegetation from her quick glance seemed to be mainly weeds. Maybe the place was abandoned. Running on along a paved path, Stewart took a moment to look behind but saw no one. As she turned back, she tumbled to the ground, her foot catching on something.

Her arms were the first part of her to feel the cold of the snow before she started to lift herself back up to her feet. As soon as she did, Stewart felt a chill across her torso as the wind combined with the layer of snow attached to her top. Then her legs felt the cool but less so, her track bottoms not being as tight to her skin. She needed shelter. But far away from here.

Maybe she could get to a road and flag down a passing motorist. Then she could get everyone back to the stately home behind her and they could get the case solved. Just maybe they could rescue Eiger. No, he was as good as dead.

Stewart could feel the tears beginning and her vision became blurred. Although Stewart worked in a job where death was a common thing to see, Eiger's sacrifice was particularly immediate. She was the police officer; she should have protected him. And yet, she knew she could not have saved him. There were too many of them, she did not have a choice, and his plan had been a good one. Heck, she was here, was she not?—with a chance of escape.

The garden ended abruptly in a wall and Stewart looked left and right but found the wall stretched both directions into the darkness. At the moment her body was still functioning well, be it the adrenalin or the terror, but she knew it would weaken as she became colder. Grabbing what looked like some loose vines, Stewart pulled at them and realised they would take her weight. Using the vegetation for purchase, Stewart clambered up the wall and jumped into a large drift of snow on the other side. Before her she saw a forest, a myriad of trees with small branches jutting out that would make passage through them difficult for her. But also difficult for her pursuers. And she was sure they would come.

It took Stewart an hour to walk through the tightly packed trees before she found a path. Her arm felt numb and her teeth were beginning to chatter. In the distance she had heard at least one dog. That was going to be an issue. But she had stumbled on, even when, from time to time, her eyes watered with tears for Eiger.

The path was four persons wide and was a well-worn track amongst the trees and Stewart realised she could cover ground quickly following it. Her arms were scraped by the trees she had brushed past giving her a patchwork of little nicks on her arms. Her right knee was sore from her feet not finding a smooth surface and the occasional hole in the ground had surprised her. With these things in mind the path looked inviting.

But with it came the risks. There was snow here among the trees, but it was not deep and her pursuers would surely use paths like this to try and find her. Her watch was showing midnight and she wondered if Sergeant McGrath would be getting worried about her. How far had she managed to tail the van? Would there already be a plan formulating? No, why would there be? It was only midnight.

Stewart wondered what the temperature was. If she stayed out here and did not find shelter, she would soon become susceptible to hypothermia and may die of exposure. It was possible for the temperature to drop quickly, especially if the cloud cover cleared. At the moment it seemed to be holding as there was no light from the moon but that could change.

Stewart shivered. God, she was cold. Looking down she saw her lace on her trainer was untied and she reached to try and fix it. But she found her hands unable to grasp the lace. Stewart breathed hard. Earlier she had applauded her fitness level but now she felt like every breath was hard work. Maybe she should stop. No, she should go quicker, try to heat up.

Pausing by the path side, Stewart stood with one hand on her knee and tried to think. If she had her glasses on, she might just have pushed them up the bridge of her nose. *You're becoming hypothermic, Kirsten. You need shelter and warmth.* Stewart looked around. *Never a cottage when you need one. Never a smiling happy woodsman with a roaring fire nearby.*

Looking along the path, Stewart thought she saw an opening in the trees. Forcing herself to move again, she made her way along the path to where she saw a small worn track in the ground. *Sheep trail. That might work.* Without really knowing why, Stewart stumbled along the track, her arms now wrapped around her, hands running up and down their length in an attempt to stay warm.

Stewart realised the trees were coming to an end. Close to where the track was, she saw the ground dip down and a stream was before her. *Dogs, if they have dogs then the water will scare them off. Always works in films. Need to walk the river for a bit.*

Stewart splashed into the river which was running slowly but which was also extremely cold. Her shoes became saturated as she waded through water up to her ankles and made her way downstream. By now Stewart had no idea where she was and any ideas she may have had were lost in the fog of the hypothermic reaction she was having.

Somewhere, I need somewhere, so cold. Got to get to somewhere. Find Macleod, tell him what I've seen. Find McGrath, crying over her tiny scar. Look at my bloody arms. And she stands there wailing about her scar. Like they are looking at your face. Wish she were here, and him. And Ross and the rest.

From the corner of her eye, Stewart saw a small patch of ground surrounded by a low wall. Stumbling out of the stream, she slipped on the low bank and landed face first in the snow. Picking herself up, she fought to get her legs moving forward and eventually reached the wall.

It was waist high and she sat down on it, ignoring the snow on top. Her track bottoms were so wet it made no difference. She could feel that her underwear was wet through too. Looking at the ground the wall surrounded, she saw that there was turned over soil with a light covering of vegetation. The vegetation was rotting but it was also interspersed with snow. *A small cottage garden*, Stewart surmised, smiling broadly for no reason. *How quaint.* Her eyes drifted to the edges of the wall and she saw a black conical piece of plastic which appeared just above the wall on the far side.

Stumbling round to it, Stewart saw it was a compost bin. *That's nice. Bit out of the way but I guess it must be fun in the summer. But the tress and the ground would bring midges, I bet.* Stewart opened the lid of the bin. A degree of steam hit her face. Maybe steam was wrong, but there was definitely heat there. Certainly, more heat than there was out here.

Come on Kirsten, time to sleep. Stewart climbed into the bin, slipping twice as she fought to co-ordinate her limbs. As she worked her way into the compost, she felt the warmth of the material but also of some things crawling around. But she didn't care. Gently she placed the lid back on top but could not close it fully.

Heat, she thought, *so good.* And then she drifted off.

Chapter 15

Hope was sitting in her car when she saw the clock change to two in the morning. Her gut was telling her something was wrong. There should not have been a problem as everything had appeared so seamless with Eiger's contact. The van had appeared on time and there had been no awkward moments as far as Hope could see from her moving car. The pick-up point had been so remote she could not park up easily without being seen and so had kept driving past until she saw the pair stepping into the back of the van.

Hope had expected Stewart to be dropped off maybe around midnight or slightly after. But there had been no word. Hope knew Stewart had no mobile on her, another enforced precaution, but she would be able to call easily enough once she had returned. Eiger's car was still at the drop off point. What bothered Hope was that she had not seen the direction the van had taken because she had to keep driving past instead of stopping. Now she had no idea where Stewart had gone.

The local radio station was on low volume in the car as Hope tried to distract herself and a song entitled 'Waiting for Someone to Come Find Me', rang out. It had that Christmas feel with the bells and the panpipes giving the main accompaniment to a driving melody.

Christmas, thought Hope, *how the hell did it get to Christmas? Looks like a lonely one this year. At one point, I thought I'd be spending it with Allinson but at least I got rid of that jerk. Maybe I'll get a sympathy dinner from the boss with Jona being away to family.* Her hand raised up to her face. *Saved a life, that's what Stewart said. Get over myself. Maybe she's right. I can't change this.*

With the vanity mirror pulled down in front of her, Hope examined in detail the scar on her face. It had healed up as much as it was going to, according to the doctors. They had offered possible plastic surgery but there were no guarantees about how inconspicuous they could make the wound appear. It might be covered but Hope's face might look significantly different to the way it had initially been.

Too many people had been scarred this year. Macleod's Jane when she got hit by that bus and then when Hope had saved her from that madman in their bathroom. Mackintosh, when she had her cancer. Stewart, when she had tried to catch that girl in Newcastle. And Macleod from the sheer weight of everything. These days the boss looked tired and yet he was still trying to sort her out. Next year should be better.

The station DJ announced it was two-thirty in the morning and Hope decided enough was enough. She called the station and found Macleod still at his desk.

'Macleod, what's the news?'

'She's not back yet, sir. I'm not content this hasn't gone wrong. I think we should start a low-level search,' said Hope; her voice slightly cracked as she spoke.

'Where do we search?'

'Well, I would say but I did not see the van she was in leave. I had to keep on the move as the location of the pick out was wide open. They could be anywhere.'

'Van licence plate?'

'I ran it as soon as I got it, but it is attached to a 2008 Volkswagen Beetle. But we could put it out anyway in case any of the nightshift see it.'

Hope could hear Macleod getting to his feet and she imagined him walking to his window, shaking a disappointed head at the view. 'We need to keep it low key in case there's anyone on the inside. We could have lives in danger. I'll ready a forcible entry team here at the station in case we need to go in quick and heavy anywhere.'

'Yes, sir. I'll wait here in case she shows up.'

'I'm going to take a look at Haskins's and Stones's homes, see if they are in. I'll also run past Kylie Magee's, see if she is there. Our best bet is that van at the moment. Otherwise, we have nothing. Let's see what we can dig up on it. I'll be in touch, Hope.'

Macleod waved a hand at Ross, asking him into the office and Macleod saw the man was exhausted. Ross had slept less than four hours since this all began, even less than Macleod. But there was no time for any sentiment as one of their own was missing. Detailing the van number plate and description to Ross, Macleod grabbed his coat and then shouted at one of the uniformed officers on the nightshift.

'Can you drive?'

'Yes, sir,' said a young female officer.

'Good, here's my keys; get a coat; we're going out.'

Macleod's first call was to the house listed as Stones's address, but he found it to be in total darkness. It was a small flat and Macleod wondered if Stones actually lived there or just used it as a pad to disappear off to. When he thundered on the door, all Macleod got back was some foul abuse from a neighbour.

'That arsehole's never here. Some bloody detective you are if you can't see that. Never darkens the door, so shut the hell up with the banging.'

If there had been more time Macleod would have had words, but he was up against it as it was. Driving to the Rehabilitated Offenders Trust, Macleod saw the place was in darkness but insisted on taking a look around the building. But there was nothing unusual and when he returned to the car, the uniformed officer driving him advised that Sergeant McGrath had reported in that she still had not seen DC Stewart.

Macleod instructed his driver to take him to the home of Dermott Haskins and he saw the same pillars surrounding the door he had earlier that night. Ringing the doorbell with an impatience, Macleod stamped his feet against the cold. He was too readily aware that Stewart could be out there in this freezing night. Earlier the stars, had been hidden behind a blanket of cloud but now they were shining bright, the clear skies causing the temperature to drop even further.

'Inspector, you find me at a breathless moment,' said Eleanor Haskins on opening the door. The woman was standing in a t-shirt with a logo across it that read 'frisky'. She was indeed out of breath and her hair was asunder, but Macleod had no time for any games.

'Sorry to bother you and pull you away from . . . your activities but I need to know, has your husband been home?'

'Inspector, if my husband were home, I would be sending him down to open this door to a man in the night. No, he's not back, probably humping some professional trollop.'

The irony of the statement was not lost on Macleod, but he needed help. 'If he comes back in, call me, privately on this number.' Macleod handed over one of his cards. 'Any time of the day. It's particularly important.'

'You look tired, Inspector. I'd offer you a brandy inside, but you have someone in the car and well, I have company as you know. Pity, really.'

'Have you been out tonight?'

'I can definitely say I have not, Inspector. Hughie has kept me quite busy.'

'When he comes home, Mrs Haskins. You have my thanks.'

'Not yet, Inspector, but we can arrange a time.' Macleod shook his head as he left. Earlier the woman had been intoxicating in her absurd way but right now she was a pain in the backside. He needed some straight talking and answers, not a teasing parley.

Stepping back into the passenger seat, Macleod gave the address for Kylie Magee and sat back to think. There was nowhere else to go with this. He was chasing any thread he had but he was not sure any would be attached to his missing DC. As the car sped across Inverness, he suddenly felt sick. He remembered the short, uniformed officer with the glasses he had seen on Lewis, her brisk manner and slightly know-it-all attitude. There had been something engaging about Kirsten and he had taken a real shine to the girl in a way he had not with Hope. His Sergeant had pulled at strings which the lack of a partner for years had left him with, but Stewart had a mind that he truly warmed to. And now she was out there somewhere, hopefully alone. And, he prayed, not fighting for her life, or lying in a ditch.

He might have just raised the entire neighbourhood with how hard he rapped the knocker on Kylie Magee's door, but Macleod did not care. After waiting for a moment, he rapped again and started a tirade against the door that lasted until it opened.

Kylie Magee stood in her dressing gown looking at the Inspector with disbelieving eyes.

'What the hell—it's like flaming four in the morning.'

'Have you been in all night?'

'What sort of question is that?'

'I'm not messing, Mrs Magee, just answer. Have you been here all night?'

'Yes, I have.'

'And can anyone prove that.'

'They can but they might not want to.' Immediately Macleod stepped back from the door and looked up to the upper level of the house. He saw the slight opening in the curtains from what he supposed was an upstairs bedroom.'

'Who is it?' Macleod asked Kylie.

'Sonny King. As you know I use his body from time to time. His mind's too small to entertain but he's good with the physical thing and too dumb to know when he's being played.'

'Get him down here.'

'Why? You know it's him.' Kylie stood with a hand on her hip and Macleod saw the legs of the woman coming out from underneath the short gown. They were perfectly toned with strong muscles.'

'I didn't make a request. If you don't go and get him, I'll come in. I need to talk to him.'

'Suit yourself, makes no difference to me; he's spent for the night anyway. I was just letting him sleep until morning.' Kylie saw Macleod's scowl. 'He might have bought me breakfast, Inspector.' With that she disappeared back into the house and a minute later Sonny King stood before Macleod.

'Are you aware of any fights tonight?'

'No,' said the man but he seemed to have to think about the answer. 'Have you asked Gordon Stones?'

'Why would I ask Gordon Stones?'

The large man froze and Macleod could see that Sonny was beginning to panic. 'Because Gordon likes fights, you see.'

'Don't you?'

'Yes, but I only go to legal ones.'

'Unlike Gordon?'

'Yes . . . I mean, no, you tricked me.' Macleod did not think this was any high praise of his talents but at least he knew what Gordon Stones was doing.

'Where is Gordon Stones?'

'I don't know.'

'You don't know where the fight is scheduled?'

'I never know where the fight is scheduled?'

'Get changed, Sonny. You're coming down to the station with me.'

'No, I'm not.' With that Sonny threw a jab at Macleod which caught him on the chin and sent him reeling backwards. His feet slipped from under him and Macleod was left sprawling on the snow-covered ground. Flipping over, he saw Sonny King, in his boxer shorts, run past the police car but he was intercepted by the young officer with her nightstick. When he refused to stop at her warning, the officer swung the nightstick and watched it bounce off King's torso before she was pushed roughly backwards and hit her head off the car. Macleod had just about got to his feet when Sonny disappeared out of sight.

Running to his colleague, he saw that she was knocked out but breathing. A voice shouted from the house. Macleod looked back to see Kylie Magee standing in front of her door, holding her gown against the cold.

'Ambulance, get an ambulance,' cried Macleod. Lights were coming on in the houses next to Mrs Magee's and soon a woman ran out in her long dressing gown, carrying a green box in one hand.

'I'm a nurse; is she badly hurt?'

'Unconscious, but breathing,' said Macleod. 'But I think there may be bleeding behind her head.' As if on cue the snow behind the officer started staining a deep red.

'Here,' said the neighbour, placing a pad in Macleod's hand and then jamming it against the officer's head. 'Just hold it steady and with a bit of force while I see what's up. Have you called an ambulance?'

Macleod nodded and although he held his hand tight to the officer's crown, he was miles away. Sonny King knew something. Maybe he was a link rather than just a dumb fighter. With his free hand, Macleod called the station and asked for all units to begin to search around his location for Sonny King. This was becoming messy, far too messy.

Chapter 16

Ross was starting to yawn; never a good sign, especially on the nightshift when morning was arriving. Well, morning by the clock anyway as the sun did not officially recognise daytime for a good few hours. But the people who got things ready would be out and about, on their buses to work, opening up and letting the nightshift go. That was what Ross missed about being in the uniform section of the police. There was always an end of shift. Sure, you might get delayed a bit but on the Murder Investigation Team you did not stop until all ends were exhausted or you caught the killer.

He looked at the coffee jug and believed that if he had one more, he would spend the rest of the day on the toilet waiting for his bladder to endlessly empty. It might keep you awake but you paid the price for the black liquid.

Ross was looking over the files again, searching for a clue as to where the fight would have taken place last night, but he had drawn a blank. In reality, the person for this job was Stewart but she was . . . just delayed. That was it, Kirsten was out there somewhere.

Being the junior members on the team, the pair had struck up quite a camaraderie and Ross knew inside he was worried.

Things did not look good. Often when things went wrong, they went spectacularly wrong. But not this time. Not to wee Kirsten. She'd lamp him one for calling her that, but she was like the baby on the team. And yet, Ross recognised she had the detective skills of Macleod, but utilised in the realms of data rather than in visual perceptions.

A call came in and Ross picked up the telephone. Macleod had been involved in a scuffle and he would be delayed coming back. In the meantime, Ross was to get all cars near Macleod's area to start looking for Sonny King. After enquiring if Macleod was okay, to which he got a condescending 'of course, I'm okay' and thereby making the point twofold, Ross called the Sergeant's desk in the station and got a description out to all cars. As soon as he put the phone down, there was a call from the incident control room in Glasgow. A body had been found in the shopping centre in Inverness. ID showed the man to be Angus Fischer.

Ross called Macleod and advised him of the development, to which Ross was told to proceed immediately and Macleod would join him as soon as possible. Grabbing some of the uniforms from the Investigation room, Ross wearily dragged himself to the car and set out for the centre.

The centre was located in the middle of Inverness and was a large development that crossed the main road into the centre. Access was through an underground car park or by a covered walkway from a nearby supermarket. Ross got his small team to park in the car park and they rode the lift up to the upper level of the retail area. Walking along the concourse, he saw a large mock-up of Santa's house and outside the front door, stood a janitor shaking his head and two police officers who waved Ross over as soon as they saw him.

'Inside there, Ross,' said a Sergeant. 'Where's the Inspector?'

'In the wars. He'll be here soon enough. How stretched are we?'

'We'll we have most of our cars combing for your colleague but as we don't know where to look it's a rather large and thankless task. I have enough people here to secure the area, so we'll be fine. I'm advising them not to open the shops until later this afternoon.'

'Okay, we'll see what Miss Nakamura thinks when she gets here. I don't know how long she'll take.'

'Of course,' said the Sergeant, 'but there will be hell on if they keep this place shut for too long at Christmas.'

Ross nodded and stepped beyond the Sergeant to the door of the tent that served as the home of Father Christmas. Inside, there was an array of lights and a fake fireplace beside which was an old rocking chair. It was motionless but contained a red suited man with a large white beard. The beard looked to have been yanked sideways at some point and Ross wondered if any of the white threads of the beard had come off on whoever had killed the festive hero.

Ross donned a glove and gently pulled the beard down and saw Angus Fischer, a man he had been speaking to only the previous evening. From what Ross could see there was no sign of a struggle other than the beard. Had Angus known his attacker? The man had been pretty spooked when they spoke, and Macleod was convinced someone had been listening to their conversation.

Stepping back out of the tent, Ross saw Jona Nakamura approaching and smiled at the Asian woman. There were times in life that you met genuinely sweet people and for Ross, Jona was one of these rare figures. Despite the gory line of work, she had none of the testy and fiery nature of her previous boss, Mackintosh, but she had all of the former's passion and skill for their art.

'Tell me you haven't been messing?' smiled Jona as she approached.

'Of course not, but I'm saying strangled as before and knew his killer. I'm going to hunt for CCTV imagery while you get a look at the body. The boss will be here soon, and he'll want answers so better get to it.'

'Anything on Kirsten?' asked Jona.

Ross shook his head and he saw the smile fade from Jona's face. 'She'll be fine,' said Ross, but not believing a word he was saying.

The janitor took Ross to a small booth that contained all of the CCTV images and when Ross saw it was a standard system, he thanked the man and asked to be left in peace. There were good recordings of all access points to the centre and Ross believed that no one could have reached the tent without being seen by the camera. It was just a matter of looking at the footage.

He ran through the pictures closest to the tent and he saw shoppers come and go with the late-night opening. Then janitors came past but soon there was little activity on the floor. The access was still open to allow people to cross through the centre and out the other side but there was no one there by eleven o'clock. Ross then spotted a figure on the move. As the lights began to be switched off, someone was moving in the dark towards the Santa house mock-up.

They were using the shadows, but Ross zoomed in on a grainy picture and examined the image. The image was in colour but the figure was in black. A cloak and a mask. It moved into the tent before emerging some three minutes later. Ross followed it on the camera and found a van waiting for the masked figure as he left. But the number plate was obscured, whether by tape of some other object. Ross sought other images but nothing gave a clear number plate.

Macleod opened the door of the camera booth and Ross pulled up the appropriate images. But as he did so, he noticed that Macleod was sporting a bruise on his chin and it looked like a peach.

'That from Sonny King, sir?' Macleod nodded. 'No wonder you want him. Anything from the Sergeant?'

'No, Ross, but our best hope is to get this case blown wide open so we know who to target to get Stewart back. She's still out there, trust me.'

Ross nodded but Macleod had not sounded convincing. The tension in the man's voice and even the tremble when he said her name was palpable and that was not common for the wise, old detective. Ross thought Macleod was almost aging before his eyes such was the strain, but the man remained focused.

'Get an idea of the man's height, Ross. I know we don't see much of his muscles but that does not look like one of our rehabilitated offenders. I'd put my money on Haskins or Stones, but you can never tell. Get Jona on to it. Tell her I want an idea as soon as possible.'

The door opened, and a quiet voice announced, 'You can tell her yourself. I have a briefing for you, Inspector, as soon as you are available.'

'I'm with you now, Miss Nakamura. Ross, get this all tidied up and over to Jona as soon as you can. I need somewhere to run with this.'

* * *

Jona Nakamura stood beside the body of Angus Fischer and pointed to the rear of the tent. 'Through there they came; there's fibres from the cloak they were wearing. At some point near the rear, they strangled Mr Fischer and then dragged him up to the rocking chair and sat him down. They probably tidied him up but someone forgot to sort out the beard. There may be fibres on the cloak from the beard or whatever was on their arms. There are no fingerprints as far as I can tell. I'll try and get footprints or rubber soles residue but to be honest it'll be hard to prove who it belongs to or at least why they were in here without good reason. How many people traipse through here?'

Macleod nodded. 'It could have been Kylie Magee and that's why Sonny King ran. He was with her and maybe he thought I had rumbled them. Of course, it could be something else. Ross thought the figure did not look like a fighter, someone of a smaller stature but who obviously can still take someone out if they want to. But why? Was it the fighting ring? If so, how is Kylie Magee involved?'

'Well, that's your department, Inspector. I will get analysis done as quickly as I can, but it will take a bit of time. Hazel is coming in to assist this morning. I wasn't going to ask her but when she heard about Stewart, she would not take no for an answer.'

'Thank you, Jona. I know everyone wants to see Kirsten safe and well, but I have a feeling she'll be the one to save herself. We are very in the dark on this one. I hope she has had the sense when to run if there was trouble.'

Macleod stepped back outside the Santa house tent and reached for his mobile. Hope had returned to the station to coordinate the search for Stewart, but she had nothing when Macleod called. The helicopter was available but where did they look? Nothing could be done overtly in case Stewart was merely late and still in the company of the operators of the illegal fights. Kurt Eiger as well as Stewart could be put into danger if they knew Kirsten was a police detective.

Macleod's mobile rang and he saw a number he recognised. He was not in the mood for the call, but he knew he would have to take it and listen to the theatrical woman on the other end.

'Inspector, I have some news for you. You asked when my husband would be home. Well, he still has not returned but I have an address you might try.'

'Did you not have this address before, Mrs Haskins,' asked Macleod, trying to not sound aggrieved at having to take the call.

'No, Inspector, I think it must have slipped my mind.' An address was passed which Macleod looked at with just a hint of scepticism.

'I take it Hughie has departed then, Mrs Haskins. Not wanting your husband home too soon. I take it that was why I did not get this address earlier.'

'How very perceptive of you, Inspector.'

'I'm running a murder investigation, so listen up good, Mrs Haskins. You fail to give me information at the appropriate time in future and I will haul you into the station and throw the book at you. I don't appreciate someone messing me about.'

'Well, then,' came the smooth reply, 'why did you become a policeman?' And the call was ended by Mrs Haskins.

Generally, Macleod did not swear but right now he came darn close. But the young officer standing at a loose end in the shopping centre certainly understood Macleod was pissed as he received a barked order to get Macleod a car and to hop to it.

Dalmore Castle was situated approximately ten miles out of Inverness on the southern side of the Moray Firth. It had an airport nearby and was currently in the hands of a London owner who was known to make only infrequent trips to his purchase. However, the place was the scene of several loud parties and many noise complaints had been made about it by the local village. But things had never come to much as connections with government and local industry leaders always seemed to smooth things over.

The driveway to the house indicated a speed limit of ten miles an hour but as the young driver of the police car slowed down, Macleod hammered his fist on the dashboard and demanded that full speed ahead was resumed. As the car pulled up at the large double doors of the castle, Macleod leaped out and began to bang loudly on the gigantic brass knocker. After a minute, the door opened, and a butler stood looking down at Macleod.

'There is a doorbell, sir.'

'Detective Inspector Macleod and if I want the results of my eye inspection, I'll send you an email, sunshine. I want Dermott Haskins now. This is a police murder investigation, and your assistance will be noted, as will any obstruction, however small.' Macleod stared fiercely at the elderly butler who simply stepped to one side.

'As this is a police matter, sir, I respectfully inform you that Mr Haskins is indisposed at this time. But in light of your comments, I will add that he is indisposed on the third floor.'

'Where on the third floor?'

'Take the stairs directly ahead, sir, and when you reach the third floor, simply turn right. He will be in one of those rooms, sir. His is the third but I cannot guarantee that he has slept in it.'

The man has obviously been a butler for a long time and knows the lay of the land, thought Macleod and tore off up the stairs. As he reached the third floor, he thought about going to Haskins's room first but with what the butler had said ringing in his head, Macleod decided he was simply going to have a clear-out.

The first door was half open but Macleod shoved it anyway and marched into the room. On his left was a girl, maybe late teens, snorting something at a table. Macleod had seen plenty of druggies in his time and was not shocked by the behaviour but her complete nudity took him slightly aback. He turned from her to see an older man trying to hide behind the bed that took up the centre of the room. His bare buttocks gave him away.

There was an adjoining door which lay open to another room and inside the picture was similar. The age of the woman was increased, and the man was a lot younger, but the activities were similar. Behind him, Macleod could hear the commotion as his officers filled the rooms, but he was wanting only one person. It was at the fifth bedroom in the row that Macleod found his man.

As he walked into the room, Macleod saw a girl standing in an outfit fit for a top shelf magazine, standing with a whip and shouting at a man. The man was naked except for a hood which covered his face. His arms were tied up to a chain that fell down from the ceiling.

'Tell me my name, weasel!' yelled the girl at the naked man and cracked the whip. Macleod flinched when he saw where she was striking.

What on earth is the world coming to? thought Macleod but he had no intention on seeing a funny side to this discovery. Stewart was still missing.

'Get out and get some decent clothes on!' ordered Macleod. The girl turned round, and despite being plastered in makeup, he saw a young face. As she walked past him, he shouted over his shoulder, 'Check that girl's age, constable. And get some female colleagues up here to assist.'

He had heard the voice of the man in bondage only once, but he knew who it was. Ripping off the mask, he saw a heavily sweating Dermott Haskins. On the table was a bag of white powder.

'Where's your clothes, Haskins? You're coming to the station.'

Chapter 17

S tewart woke with a start and then found her arms and legs severely restricted. They were not bound but instead she could not move them outwards beyond a certain point. Bringing them in towards her was not easy but at least it was possible. Gradually she made herself a small area where she could shift her limbs back and forth and drive the pins and needles in them away.

Something was also moving down her back. It was like a fly crawling along. And something else was on her neck moving down towards the nape and under her top. Realisation of where she was drifted slowly into Stewart's mind and she held herself together despite the small creatures that were moving under her clothing.

Slowly, she raised herself upwards until her head cleared the compost she was immersed in. She was warm, or at least not freezing, and she worked a hand towards her chest and then upwards until she touched the lid of the container she was in. Cautiously, she pushed that lid upwards. Sunlight streamed in and the sounds of the world followed it.

There was a bird call, trilling along. A robin? Kirsten was no expert, but she recognised the familiarity of the call at least. There was the sound of an aeroplane overheard too. If she was still in her former locality then that was the airport approach as the sound of the engines was too close to be a high-flying aircraft. There was a crunch of footsteps too in snow and Stewart felt suddenly chilled inside but not from the cold.

Where was Kurt Eiger? Had they killed him already? She was running for help, running to bring someone else back to free him. A morbid thought ran across her mind and she saw him on the metal floor of the arena, blood oozing from his head.

Again, she heard footsteps crunch the snow. Was it her pursuers, or was it a simple walker, someone she could go to for help? One would bring salvation, the other, a death sentence. Deciding she could not risk it, Stewart remained within the compost bin she had climbed into and listened as the crunch of feet became quieter. There was nothing to do but wait.

Surely the Sergeant would have acted by now, sent everyone after Kurt Eiger and her. She was going to follow them so she would know where Stewart was. Had she managed that? Kirsten thought back to the start of the previous night. The pick-up point had been incredibly open, hard to hide nearby. And then she had been in the van, blindfolded and unsure of where she was. She had heard an aeroplane so that tallied but otherwise, Stewart had no idea where she was.

She had gone through the river or stream. Memories of her actions after she had fled were somewhat faded, probably from the cold. She had been wet and stumbling along. Now she was wet but at least she was also warm. If she got out of the compost she would start to become cold again. Yes, there were sunny skies from the little she saw but that meant a cold hard frost as well as the snow which had already fallen. She would need help or more shelter quickly if she were not to freeze outside.

This was a place of relative safety, she reckoned. Inside the compost, her smell would be disguised so if any dogs came and had the scent, she would be safe unless they got really close. *That was how it worked, wasn't it? Or do I gamble and go for the road, wherever that is.*

Stewart decided that she needed to assess her situation from outside the compost bin where at least she could see the lay of the land. Slowly, she raised herself up in the bin and pushed the lid upwards so she could peer out. There were no untoward sounds just the occasional call of birds and the noise of the road in the distance. Quickly she climbed out of the bin and replaced the lid, shaking as the cool air hit her wet clothes and body. Her stomach growled but she ignored it and sought out cover.

The bin was on the edge of a small vegetable garden which was in remission due to winter. But this garden had a low wall around it and Stewart ducked down behind it and began to scan her surroundings. Behind her was a forest, thick with trees. It seemed dark in the poor winter sun which struggled to penetrate the upper greenery and left the ground barren with a sea of browns and greys where the snow had struggled to fall through. That was an option, plenty of cover but they would surely have placed plenty of people there. The road was also through the forest, so it was an obvious escape route.

Before her were crop fields, large and open. Between each was a low hedge or line of trees but the fields themselves were just a white blanket. As Stewart looked from field to field, she saw that one seemed to have snow that was slightly higher than it should be. Maybe her eyes were just struggling, after all she had her contacts in. They were as good as her glasses for close in viewing but at longer distances they could take a toll on the eyes. Stewart had slept in them so they were hurting.

Blinking and then refocusing on the field in question, Stewart realised that the snow looked higher because there was a cover over the field. Well at least it was there in small rows. A whirr filled the air and Stewart glanced around until she saw the light aircraft about a thousand feet up and routing towards what must be the airport. Maybe she was close to the approach path. Beyond the fields she thought she saw the Moray Firth and so she reckoned she was east of the airport.

A thought struck Stewart. If she could disturb the covered field, she could leave a message the pilots on approach to the airport might see and relay. But what could she leave? She would not have all day to simply prepare a message. This was not some castaway situation, simply awaiting a passing vessel. If she left the message then her pursuers might see it too, provided they did not catch her in the act to begin with. She had no idea how many people were after her. This way she could leave a message even if she were caught afterwards.

The field was maybe a quarter of a mile away and Stewart traced the hedgerows down to it. If she stayed low and close to them, she might just get there without being seen. And then she heard a noise behind her. It was footsteps and two men having a conversation.

'He's not going to like this. It's like she just vanished. The guys on the perimeter are going to get it.'

'Feisty girl too. Derek said she had a bit of spunk in her, looked ready to fight. Pity about Kurt. He took me on, but he never saw where the money was. He was a dead man walking after Davie died.'

'Okay but don't go there. You know he might be anywhere here, and we don't talk about that, do we?'

The voices were now close, and Stewart remained hunkered down behind the wall. Her fists closed and she prepared herself for a fight if it came to it. She was stiff and feeling like anyone would, having been curled up in a bin for the night, but the casual conversation about Kurt Eiger had given her enough fire in her belly.

'Anyway, she's not here. There's nowhere to hide and the footprints on the path could be made by anyone now. Bloody dogwalkers are all over this place.'

There are no dog footprints though, thought Kirsten, *these guys would never make a detective*.

Stewart heard the men walk away, their feet crunching through the snow. They must have come close but not close enough to see the footprints beside the bin perhaps. Maybe others had come by in the night while she was in the bin. Regardless, she would need to make a move. If they came here once, they could always retrace their steps to search again.

Lifting her eyes above the wall, she saw the men had gone but kept still for another two minutes to see if anyone else was around. Once she was confident no one else was there, Stewart ran quickly from the vegetable garden to the nearest field and the hedgerow at the side of it. She kept low and crouched but was aware she was leaving footprints behind.

The opposite side of the hedge was another field and Stewart did not wait to see what was behind it. The air felt colder as she ran but this was from her wet clothing. In the compost bin she had been warmer, but she had never come back to a normal temperature. Now outside she was feeling the effects of not starting from a decent body temperature.

Relentlessly, Stewart ploughed on, pushing any pain or feelings of cold away from her mind. She needed to get this completed then maybe she could go back to the bin. One field was passed after another and she found herself in the one she had targeted. There were white sheets pinned down just above the surface and which now had a layer of snow on them. Each long sheet seemed to run from one end of the field to the other but was only about five feet wide.

Stewart felt the material and tried to rip it. It had a plastic feel on one side but the other felt less synthetic. At first it would not rip but she concentrated on making a tiny tear and once started it seemed to come away more easily.

But what should she spell out on the ground, the brown soil underneath her chalk on the whiteboard of the field? These would be pilots, so something simple and something they could not fail to react to. SOS! That would be it, SOS. But that could be for anyone so Stewart thought she would add something else to make sure they knew it was her. SOS and then a KS beneath it. That would do it.

Walking slowly along the perimeter hedge, Stewart found her starting mark and then ran into the field between a line of the covering fabric. It was not easy as the line available was extremely narrow, but she found her starting point and made a rip. In her mind she pictured an S but made in pixelated form. *Keep it simple, Kirsten, keep it simple.* Her hands shook with cold as she pulled at the fabric, the snow often coming off in a furry and covering her. She shivered as the wind caught on her and made the wet top feel even colder and her track bottoms clung in a damp chill to her legs.

Something kept Stewart going—the fear of death in the main as she reckoned someone would soon see her and she would then be on the run. But there was only the quiet of the countryside. Try as she might to simply concentrate, Stewart kept glancing off to the further away fields and back to the garden she had come from. But no one was visible. As she finished her work, she made her way back to the hedgerow and crouched down awaiting an aeroplane. The sound of a whirring engine made her believe it would not be a long wait.

There came a whir and her eyes squinted to see what was making the sound in the sky, a lawnmower of the air by the noise of it. Her contacts hurt, dry as her eyes were, but she saw a blur coming closer. It could only be about five hundred feet up and she saw a blue wing and beneath it a man sat in what looked like a go-kart. As the image got closer, Stewart recognised it as a microlight and stepped out of the hedge and began to wave her arms at it.

All the pilot had to do was take note of the situation and continue his approach to the airport and advise the air traffic unit who would contact search and rescue, or the police as it was inland. In her mind Stewart had this all worked out.

But the pilot had a different idea as he started to circle over the sign on the ground, coming round low. Stewart thought about shouting to him but with the noise of the propeller behind him he would hear nothing. The man seemed to just keep circling. Soon someone would realise and come towards her. Stewart glanced back at the garden to see if her run to the bin would be safe, but she saw men there already. They were not looking at the bin but rather had binoculars trained on the microlight and possibly Stewart. When they began to run towards her, her fears were confirmed. Stewart ran across the field away from her pursuers, out towards the shores of the Moray Firth.

Chapter 18

Macleod looked across the table at the garden centre owner opposite. Dermott Haskins's clothes were crumpled and his hair a mess from having been inside a leather hood while receiving admonishment from a young female. At least that was how Macleod was going to write it up in his report. Frankly, he was a dirty bugger as they would have said on the beat but his activities, sordid as they were, were not Macleod's main concern. Stewart was still missing and Macleod needed to know where the private fight had been held the previous evening. Was Dermott Haskins involved in that side? Macleod did not know but he was sure that Haskins was up to something and just maybe he knew someone involved. His relationship with Gordon Stones was an area Macleod wanted to know about and fast.

Hope was standing behind Macleod, taking up that position he had been occupying when Macleod was letting her take the lead. But now he could feel Hope almost wanting to nip over his shoulder and get a hold of this man. Just an hour ago, Hope had fielded a call from the care provider of Stewart's brother, and it seemed they had allowed him onto the call. Hope had seemed shaken when she came off the call and Macleod swore she had even shed a tear. Not that Macleod thought she was weak for doing it, quite the opposite in fact.

'When did last night's activities start?'

Haskins looked sourly at Macleod and shrugged his shoulders. 'Maybe eight o'clock; I can't remember. It was a bit of a palaver as the entertainment had got caught in the snow.'

'How do you mean, caught the snow?'

'Their mini-bus had broken down, I mean; you can ask them. So, I was kicking my heels at the house for a while. In fact, I grabbed a sleep before they arrived, hence why I was still up and at it this morning.' Macleod swore he detected a smile on the man's face.

'The girl whipping your . . ., entertaining you this morning, was barely eighteen.'

'But eighteen all the same, I am not reckless, Inspector.'

'You or your service provider? Why were you there? Did you organise this?'

'Me? How could I organise this? You need to speak to Simon Farrellsworth; it's his place, after all.'

'Farrellsworth? He's the big shot lawyer for some rather nasty people from Russia if I'm correct. Did he provide the drugs?'

'Not directly, but it was all part of the package.'

Macleod glanced back at Hope and she nodded. 'Package for what?' asked Macleod.

'Being a partner. He has a share in my garden centre chain.'

'What sort of share?'

'He's the co-owner. Of course, I do all the donkey work up here and trouble shoot all the problems and he keeps the funding coming in. It's worked well and occasionally we have a little party. Well, I do and few other businesses he's associated with. Please ring him. I could do with getting out and grabbing some lunch.'

'You're going nowhere, Haskins. Tell me, how well do you know Gordon Stones? Is he one of your partners as well?'

Haskins shook his head and stood up. 'Is there any decent coffee in here? I mean, can you get me some paracetamol and a decent latte. It was a rough night, but she was worth it. I mean you saw her, Inspector.'

'I saw a dirty pervert and a misguided girl. I saw drugs that are going to get you a jail term. Now sit down and answer the question. What is your relationship with Gordon Stones? I mean the whole lot.'

'Stones? I barely know Stones, Inspector. He was introduced to me by a Mario who works for Mr Farrellsworth as a good supplier for my Santa Clauses in the grottos this year. I have a contract to supply all the grottos, you see; it's not a great profit maker but you know what, sometimes I like to give things back to the community. I was telling Mario about my problem of recruiting Santas and he mentioned that I could do a double good to the community by employing some ex-offenders as well as cheering everyone up.'

'You didn't think ex-offenders as Santa was a bit risky? I mean, there are kids involved.'

'Everything was above board, Inspector. Until one of them died and all this headache began. In fact, I think that's why last night was so good. I needed to blow off a little steam.'

'Two of them are dead, Mr Haskins,' said Hope. 'One died last night at the shopping centre in the town. Where were you at eleven o'clock?'

'Died. Another one? This is a disaster. Can you see the press, Inspector? Santa's bumped off in the night—what will you find at the bottom of your chimney this Christmas? A fat jolly man with his neck broken. This is bad.'

'Especially for the Santa,' snapped Hope. 'Can anyone confirm you were where you said you were?'

'Of course. I think the butler let me into the room and then woke me up when the entertainment arrived so he will be aware. I mean, my car was there the whole time.'

'Is there CCTV at Dalmore?' asked Macleod.

'I don't think Mr Farrellsworth is a fan of recorded material, Inspector.'

'Do you know the whereabouts of Gordon Stones?' Hope spat the words and Macleod could see the anger behind her offering. She needed to be cooler, tough as it was.

'How could I?'

A knock came on the door and Hope popped out while a uniformed officer entered the room. A few moments later, Hope stuck her head inside again.

'She's been spotted.'

'Go get her, Sergeant!'

* * *

Stewart looked over her shoulder, but the men were still coming. In the distance she heard what sounded like a quad bike and she ran all the harder because of it. If she stuck to awkward places, it would struggle to follow.

The microlight was still circling around overhead, and she prayed he had actually told someone instead of simply watching the show. There was only one real option, to run across the fields and Stewart knew that would soon run out as she reached the shores of the Moray Firth. Maybe the services had been called and would be waiting there for her. She could not see the shoreline, but she prayed the pursuing mob would not be there, waiting. Then she could run left or right along the beach, keep the chase going until someone arrived. That was the problem now. If that microlight tailed her, they would always know where she was.

Her limbs felt tired, but she pushed them on like she was in the last round of a fight. Usually it was heat exhaustion that was the problem under lights. Here, despite all the effort she was putting in, she still felt cold as the wind hit her damp clothing.

The quad bike was getting closer, its helmeted rider strad-dled imposingly on his beast. Stewart cut past a hedge and through a small gap which would force the bike to take a different path. The sea was now clearly in view, the white of the waves evident as they crashed to shore. As she reached what might be the last hedgerow, Stewart tripped and was sent sprawling at full speed into the tiny sharp points of the hedge. She tugged herself free, her hair being pulled back and numerous scratches and cuts started to bleed. She cursed the pain she felt but her real fear was the delay the fall had caused. Now clear of the hedgerow she saw the beach and water before her, but from the corner of her eye, she saw the quad bike approaching.

Hitting the beach, Stewart made her way straight for the water, but the quad was clearly going to cut her off. As she ran, it came up behind her and she felt something wrap quickly around her legs. She crashed to the sandy surface and immediately reached down to find her legs tied up in a mess of rope with two weights.

The quad stopped and a figure came over, a massive chest

on legs like tree trunks. Stewart recognised a fighter, but she feigned an injury lying on the ground as if poleaxed. The man came over without any caution and lent over her to check her vitals. Without hesitation, she reached up and grabbed his helmet, pulling him down to her and sinking her fingers into the gap between his helmet and his neck. The helmet was ripped free and Stewart kept an arm wrapped around him. His hands flew out onto her body and she felt a hard punch to her ribs, followed by another. Seeing the man's ear, Hope bit into it with all she had, feeling the flesh rip.

The man screamed and Stewart let her arm encircle his neck and shoved two fingers into his eyes. It was dirty fighting, but this was for her life, not some simple arrest. As the man howled, Stewart pushed him off her, cleared the ropes from her feet, and started pumping her legs one more time as she went from a crouch to a run. She could hear the cries of other men and out of the corner of her eye she could see them less than fifty metres away. There was only one option left to her and Kirsten went straight for the water. The bloody microlight was still circling and she struggled to hear much as she dived into the water and began to swim.

It was a struggle against the breaking waves and her feet touched the bottom several times as she fought her way out into the deeper water. Stewart did not dare look round but simply kept swimming further and further out into the Firth. Her arms ached and she was beginning to panic as she felt her strength going. It had been a long time since she had fled the building and now the lack of proper rest and the tension which had exhausted her made her begin to feel like this might be the end. The face of her brother passed before her eyes and Kirsten felt herself choking up. How would he survive? How would he cope in this world without her? He was still a child in mind if a tall and strong man in body.

And then everything became so noisy. Even when she dipped below the water, she found her ears being assaulted with the sound of a howling wind, like a hurricane in your room. A hand grabbed her and someone said something to her. Kirsten had no idea who it was and part of her lashed out, but she was then too weak to continue. The next thing she was being lifted up in the air with a man looking at her, wearing a white helmet. He would then look up into the noise above.

The wind was cold, and she shivered involuntarily as she was taken inside a helicopter. Lying on the floor of the aircraft, she said her name when asked. 'I'm Kirsten, I'm Kirsten. Stewart, they call me Stewart.' She tried to sit up but a gentle hand pushed her back down. The cuts from the bush were stinging now, maybe from the sea water and her contacts felt like they were going to burn her eyes out. Stewart forced herself up right and stuck a finger into her open eye to remove them. A hand pushed her gently back down and her eyes were splashed with water before she found her contacts being removed.

Stewart lay there and a faint smile came across her shivering body as a blanket was placed over her. She had done it, she was clear. And Kurt Eiger? Kirsten saw the man's face and then heard him telling her to go. Without warning, she simply burst into tears.

Chapter 19

Macleod stood at his window looking at the dreaded car park view. One day he would simply get a picture and hang it across the space and gaze at something more interesting. But he was in a better mood now that Kirsten was safe. She was at the hospital being checked over and Macleod was awaiting an update on her condition and any information from Hope. But as happy as he was that his constable was now safe and secure, Macleod still had two deaths on his hands and a possible third. Kurt Eiger was still out there. Any minute, he would have the story from Stewart, and they would be on their way to try and find Mr Eiger.

Keeping the fighting ring from being exposed was clearly something worth killing for but just who knew what? Dermott Haskins was denying all knowledge of underground fights and Gordon Stones had disappeared. Sonny King was also missing and had run away from Kylie Magee's. Just who had what links to what? And why kill people in a grotto? It was like the tale of a serial killer but without the reason.

Macleod heard his telephone ring and turned quickly to grab it. 'Hope?'

'Sorry Inspector, it's Jona Nakamura. I would appreciate it if one of you could come down to the shopping centre.'

'What's the issue, Miss Nakamura? I was under the impression that you were just about cleared up.'

'I was, Inspector, but there's been a development. It appears our Santas were going to be rather generous. One of my colleagues saw a number of gifts on the floor around a small Christmas tree. They thought nothing of it but needed to move the tree in order to look for some prints. But as they moved the parcels, they were aware they were extremely heavy for what would normally be empty packages. I mean, these should have been decorative as they don't keep the real gifts in the tent overnight. You'd move them somewhere more secure.'

'Okay, but what's the point, Jona? I'm expecting an extremely important call.'

'Long story, short, there's a lot of class A drugs inside the packages, all in decorative covers, in small enough sizes to be carried away from Father Christmas while your kids get a gift as well. You're looking at a very clever drug shop right under our noses.'

Macleod was speechless. The sheer audacity of it. In front of the children too. 'Good, Jona, I believe you'll be a while longer then. I'll get uniform off to the other sites and secure them. Looks like your people might have some overtime this Christmas.'

'I hear you found Kirsten. Is she okay?'

'As far as I know. Hope is up with her at the moment.'

'And how's Hope?'

'Better, more like herself.'

'Good, I'll have you a report soon as and I'll get some teams together if you can get me the other sites to check over.'

Macleod shouted Ross through to the office and saw the man's tired eyes. 'Are you okay?'

'Are you, sir?'

'Point taken. It turns out that the Santa grottos are being used to send out drugs. Miss Nakamura's team managed to find small packets of class A drugs in parcels used for decoration inside the tents. You're on this, Ross. Sergeant McGrath will take the underground fighting line and I'll try and work out just who is involved in what. Are you okay to handle it? See Sergeant Mathers downstairs and tell him I need as many people as he can give me. After the search, it'll need to be the new shift but tell him to let the troops know this was in front of the kids, possibly their kids.'

Ross nodded. 'Any word from Kirsten?'

'Not yet but she's fine, Ross. I know the two of you are the work horses of this team and that you look out for each other. But she's fine. We'll have plenty of time to lick our wounds later. Right now, we have a missing man and a lot of drugs to clean up.'

'Sir,' said Ross and left. His usual chirpiness was gone and Macleod did not blame him. Stretching, Macleod heard something click and winced. There were days when stretching helped and others when it was too much effort.

A text message came in on his phone. There were just two words in the message from Hope. DALMORE CASTLE.

* * *

Hope had left the hospital, past the Christmas tree and the tinsel of the front door, in such a hurry she nearly clattered into a man with a broken leg on his way out. She gave a swift, 'Sorry!' over her shoulder but ran hard to her car. Stewart had said she had come from a large house near where she had ended up in the dark; her colleague had reckoned on not travelling more than about four miles if that. And judging from where they had picked Stewart up, the only house nearby of a size appropriate to hold an underground arena would have to be Dalmore House.

The fact they had been there earlier when they had arrested Haskins and his fellow party goers only added to the picture. They must have watched the fights before going on to their other entertainments. In truth, Hope saw the fights as probably more reasonable a pastime than the other sports.

The roads were treacherous until you reached the main routes which had been cleared and gritted allowing for easy passage of all the festive shoppers. Today was a Saturday and the first weekend of December so there were plenty of purchasers out and about. As she let her siren sound and the lights moved cars from her path, she realised she had so few people to buy for. Jona, really. And she might get Macleod something. But what? A tie? How bland.

The sight of an aircraft climbing above her, routing away from the airport, brought her mind back to her job and Hope concentrated on the turnings off the main road once she had passed the airport. Soon, she saw the turn for Dalmore Estate and took the long, winding road which led to the large estate house. There was still a forensic contingent there and Hope recognised Hazel Mackintosh taking the lead. The diminutive woman was a tour de force and Hope watched her round on a poor investigator who had obviously labelled something incorrectly.

'Sergeant McGrath, how can I help you?' asked Mackintosh on seeing her. 'I'm afraid we are almost completed here. Was there anything in particular you wanted?'

'I want you to find a concrete slope down to an underground metal arena.'

Mackintosh laughed. 'No seriously, Detective, how can I help you?'

Hope explained what had happened to Stewart and watched as Mackintosh's face became more and more confused.

'Not here, Sergeant. There's no concrete slope down. I did have a look round the house and I cannot see anything unusual. This house has not been altered downstairs and there is no outside access to any lower basement. I'm sorry detective but Stewart must be confused.'

Hope took a step back and looked at the house. Its form was impressive, and the long stone used to build it must have been a chore in its day. No simple crane popping along to assist. *Stewart was woozy, she admitted that,* thought Hope, *but she's not that crazy. She must have come from somewhere.*

'Is there anyone of use in the house who might know the estate?' Hope asked Mackintosh.

'There's a butler inside, quite an age but he was highly informative about the house. I think he's a bit shocked by it all. The Inspector made quite an impression on him earlier. He's in the kitchen as I remember, giving a statement.'

Hope thanked the forensic officer and then strode into the house. After grabbing a passing maid for instructions, she made her way to the kitchen and found a grey-haired man sitting in a chair breathing hard. He looked exhausted but Hope needed answers.

'Excuse me, sir, my name is Sergeant McGrath and I need a little help. I understand you have a good knowledge about this house.'

The man wearily stood up and nodded. With his hands held together he asked, 'How can I help you, ma'am?'

'I was wondering, is there a basement in this house? I mean a new one, refurbished or installed in the last few years.'

'No, ma'am. I mean there has been plenty of changes since the old master left what with these parties that are held and the women arriving in the night. It's not even just women—there's men coming in too. I really am not built for this.' The man started to shake, and Hope felt she had to help him back into his seat.

'Is there anywhere that has been developed recently on the estate?'

'Well, the new master was looking at converting the old lodge. It's quite a grand affair but it has fallen into disrepair. I believe there was some work on the building, but it's been locked up now for at least a year or two. Apparently once they had looked at the foundations there was no option other than to condemn the place. But the electric still works. I know because I have seen it some nights. But be careful if you go there because it is a ruin. It wouldn't do for a lovely woman like yourself to be injured.'

'Thank you, sir,' said Hope and then kept herself in front of the man while she made sure he was okay.

'I'm too old for this,' he said.

'I think so. Maybe find somewhere that appreciates you.'

Hope strode from the kitchen and made her way back out of the house and to her car. Grabbing an Ordnance Survey map, she sat in her front seat and scanned the estate. There was a large building identified as the lodge across from here and looking out of the window she saw it. There was a set of gardens in front of it as well and Hope thought this looked promising. As she turned the car over to start making her way across a tap came on her passenger window.

'Room for one?' said Macleod opening the door. 'Where are you going?'

'To find your fighting pit; hop in, sir.'

Hope relayed what the butler had said, and Macleod laughed when she said the butler had found Macleod rather scary.

'I was slightly pumped earlier; however, the lack of sleep is beginning to get to me. I was going to drive up but glad I didn't as I think I nodded off momentarily in the car on the way here. I did ask but the constable said I didn't.'

'As if he would say,' laughed Hope. Then, in a sudden change of tone, 'Do you think Eiger's still alive?'

'Doubtful. Too much of a risk. Did Stewart get to see anyone else at the fight?'

'Just the fighters themselves who she thought might be ex-cons as Eiger thought they nearly all seemed to be supplied these days by Stones. I'm having some of the photobooks sent over to see if Stewart can identify any of them.'

'Good. If we can find this fight pit then maybe we can get some DNA, start matching up a few things. I'm worried if we don't get to whoever's behind this they could cut and run by dispatching everyone who knows.'

Macleod's mobile rang as they arrived at the lodge building. Picking it up, he answered, and Hope got out of the car. As she walked towards the building, she heard her boss fuming behind her before he fumbled with his mobile.

'What are you doing?'

'I think the battery is playing up, so I've just taken it out to let it cool down. You can't be too careful with these devices. I've heard sometimes if they overheat, they explode.'

'Someone trying to shut us down?'

Macleod grimaced. 'I told you, the mobile is playing up. I'll need to get it fixed so we had better find this fighter's pit quickly, in case the repair team show up and try to confiscate the mobile on me. Wouldn't be good.'

Hope strode towards the lodge building and then started to circumvent it. 'Stewart said she came up a concrete slope and to a garden, so it's got to be just around here.'

She raced on ahead of her boss and found the descending slope. At the bottom of it was a metal sliding door and Hope looked around for the controls. A panel was beside the door but was covered up with a cloth. Removing the cloth, she pressed the up button, but the door failed to start. Macleod arrived and bent down and tried to grab the bottom of the door. It would not budge.

'Quick,' he said, 'get something from the car to jimmy this open.'

Hope ran back and returned a minute later with a crowbar. She stuffed the flat end under the door and started to lift it. The mechanism was strong, and Macleod helped. The door shifted slightly but Hope could feel the strain on her back. As soon as they let go, the door descended again.

'Okay,' said Macleod, 'we lift together and then you dive under while I hold it.'

'Me? Are you sure you can hold it?'

'Maybe, but I know I'll never get down low enough to slide under the door.'

The pair lifted the door again and as they reached a few feet off the floor, Hope let go, and Macleod yelled under the weight of his task. Hope did not wait and slid down, rolling under the door which promptly slammed shut just as she cleared it.

After taking a moment's breath, Hope stood up in the dark and switched on the light on the back of her mobile. Beside the door she saw another control panel and tried the up button. It began to lift, and she saw the feet of Macleod.

'Good, what's in there?'

'It's kind of dark,' said Hope, keeping her finger on the door so that as much daylight could flood in as possible.

'Over there, Hope,' said Macleod staring into the distance. I can see a door.' Hope followed him across a concrete floor and then through an archway. They stepped onto a metal floor and Macleod looked around the shiny arena. Above them was darkness and Macleod told Hope to shine the light from her phone upwards.

'It's an amphitheatre, a blasted amphitheatre. They can look down on it and enjoy the bloodletting. I thought these were things of the past,' said Macleod.

'They've done a good job cleaning though, haven't they? Stewart said there were three fights in here and the blood was flowing across the floor.'

'I'll let Miss Nakamura be the judge of how good a job they've done. Time to get her here on the double. I'll just reinstate my phone.'

'Who was calling on it before, sir? Who was trying to stop you searching here? The DCI.'

Macleod shook his head. 'Much higher, from England. Special forces he was claiming. Well, let them come. I have his number and I want to know why he was wanting this covered up.'

Chapter 20

Macleod was taking an earful from the DCI. Not because he had just ignored someone in the darker services of the country but because of the situation Stewart had found herself in originally. Macleod felt that the risk had not been as great as it had turned out but he decided rather than argue about whether he was right or wrong, he would simply let his boss speak and get it over with. In recent months, he had upset the higher echelons and then been proved right, and this was his boss unloading all the earache she had taken and defending she had done of him before senior management

But what Macleod was really waiting for was a call from Jona Nakamura. At the moment he had two murders and a missing man and nothing to tie anyone definitively to any of it. After he had received his punishment from his boss, Macleod stepped out into the main office where he saw Ross at his computer. A number of people were around him and Ross waved them away as Macleod approached.

'Making good progress, sir, on the drugs front. Been in touch with other departments and a few of the lower cogs in the wheel have spoken and there's a good case against Haskins as the main man behind this operation. But there are links higher up. With your permission, I think it's time to hand this over for the drugs team to run. At the end of the day, Haskins is going nowhere.'

'I understand, Ross, but we need full co-operation. I still have him as a suspect in our murders. The death of Angus Fischer would have suited Haskins well. Maybe he or one of his cronies saw us at Fischer's and then decided to finish him off. As for Kieran Magee, maybe he was a similar problem, but I don't know why. He never came to us and as far as I understand, he was not about to come forward and spill the beans.'

'Anything on Kurt Eiger?' asked Ross.

'McGrath's had searches of the surrounding countryside in operation but there's been nothing. Hopefully, we'll catch a break. But I think we're too late. I need Miss Nakamura to give us something.'

Macleod's mobile rang and he returned to his office to take it.

'Sir, it's Stewart.'

'Good to hear your voice, Kirsten. You gave us quite a fright.'

'I apologise, sir, but it went wrong very quickly.'

'Nothing to apologise about. I don't want to rush you but I'm expecting an important call.'

'Sure, sir, but I need to tell you. One of the goons that drove the van last night, I have spotted him in the photo books of previous criminals. He's called Hugh McGovern. Massive build of a guy; I'll send you the picture over.'

Macleod held the phone away from his ear and almost dropped it when the picture came through. 'Are you sure about this?'

'Totally, sir. They never gave their names that night but that was him, clear as day. He was driving the van. Why, sir? Do you know him?'

'Last night, he was at Mrs Haskins and she said he was there all night. Having a wild time. It doesn't make sense but I'm bringing him in, and Mrs Haskins with him.'

Macleod hung up the call and was about to call the Sergeant's desk downstairs when his mobile rang again. It was Jona Nakamura and he answered as swiftly as he could.

'We have a couple of things, Inspector. We have some black thread from a garment. I'm thinking that with the black cloak used in the Fischer killing it might be something, but I need the cloak to match it up.

'We also have a tyre tread from a van. It's quite clear but also reasonably common. If you get any abandoned vans, it might give us a good idea if it was there, but I can't guarantee anything.

'But the big discovery is a fingerprint. It's a good one and it belongs to Gordon Stones.'

'Where did you find it?'

'In the arena. He must have lent up at some point or other because it would have been above his head. I guess someone did not clean up as well as they thought. In the upper floor there are some hair samples, but they come from persons who are not on record. I can't match them to anyone we know.'

'Good work, Jona; keep me informed if there's anything else.'

Macleod strode from the office and shouted at Ross to get his jacket and some uniformed officers in cars.

'What's the issue, sir?'

'We are going to pick a few people up. Gordon Stones for one and then Mrs Haskins.'

Macleod was silent in the car on the way to the Rehabilitated

Offenders Trust. In the back of his mind he thought about the call he had received from the man purporting to be from his country's more secret services. Maybe he had been, maybe not but there was a tone to the request to remain clear that was almost pleading. Maybe Stones was in more trouble than Macleod could muster.

Macleod did not wait for an invite by the receptionist to enter into the rest of the building and stood at the front desk, telling his uniformed officers to search it. Now that he had Stones at the site of the fights, he had a lot more leeway in pursuing him. But as he stood awaiting his officers' return, he had a sinking feeling. When there was no joy with the search, Macleod asked the receptionist if there was anyone more senior he could speak to. She advised that a Mrs Bell would be down directly.

Mrs Bell was an older woman, maybe late sixties, who wore an old fashioned but plain skirt and jumper with a string of pearls. She had maintained her hair as best she could, but the colour was fading, and it was clearly thinning.

'Inspector, what can I do for you?'

'What is your role here, Mrs Bell?' asked Macleod.

'Well, I basically take care of the day-to-day paperwork. As you can imagine with a trust like ours, there are a large number of forms going back and forward; there's also expenses to be paid. Mr Stones is very much the figurehead, but he needs someone to keep the ship steady.'

Macleod tried to size the woman up but found that she showed no sign of lying. Maybe she was a genuine operator in this charity. Had Stones been using it for his own gain?

'Has there been anything unusual today, apart from Mr Stones non-attendance at the centre?'

'That's not unusual, Inspector. He's often away for a couple of days. What is remarkable is that there was a large amount of money deposited into our account this morning. Almost nine hundred thousand pounds. It's from an account I don't recognise. I was going to call the bank as it must be a mistake.'

Macleod stepped away and sat down on one of the chairs in the reception area. What was going on? Everything just seemed so confusing.

'Have you heard from Sonny King at all, Mrs Bell? Has he been here recently?'

'Not in the last day or so, Inspector. He's a frequent visitor and a favourite of Mr Stones.'

Macleod needed to get hold of these suspects, but they were certainly not around. He spoke to his uniformed detail and asked them to check the last known addresses again of the suspects. But as Ross drove him back to the station, he was in a sombre mood.

As they approached the station, Macleod's mobile rang, and he saw it was the Sergeant's desk. 'Macleod.'

'Inspector, you need to get up to the Kessock Bridge; we have a jumper.'

'Hardly my forte, sergeant.'

'I believe it's Gordon Stones, sir. And he's asking for you.'

Ross spun the vehicle in the car park and raced out to the A9 and drove to the Kessock Bridge. There was single file traffic in progress and Macleod could see two uniformed officers, watching a man dressed in a Santa Claus outfit. As Ross parked the car as close as he could, Macleod strode up the police line and watched it break apart for him. He addressed the officer at the bridge. 'What's happening, constable?'

'He says his name is Gordon Stones and that he wanted to

speak to you, sir. Other than that, we have not had a word from him, but he has leant over if we as much as step towards him.'

'Okay, officer, I'll deal with it from here.'

The Kessock Bridge was the impressive metal fixture that carried cars from one side of the Moray Firth at Inverness, over to the Black Isle. It gave a glorious view of the firth itself and sat beside the local football club, but Stones had chosen to stand precariously on the side facing Inverness and the site of the old ferry. As Macleod got closer, he saw that Stones had a full Santa Claus outfit on and there was a rope around his neck which had a long amount of play, lying at his feet. But the other end was tied tight to the bridge's railing.

'Inspector, when I first saw you, I said to Sonny, "This will be the end of the fights."'

'So, you admit you set them up?'

'I was the master of the ring, Inspector, but I was not the brains. Oh, no, there are many higher up than me. You won't have found them, and they won't admit to anything. Your girl, she saw some of them, but they were all masked. One of the rules so they can bring people with them, but no one sees anyone else. They even bring in the staff from elsewhere, their own collection. I was responsible for getting the talent together. It started off quietly enough, just a bit of a rougher brawl like happens in numerous parts of the country. But these people wanted more, and they offered big money. Some of the guys at the Trust, they struggle to get by, struggle to hold a real job because all they know is how to give someone a beating. So, we turned it into a recruiting ground. Our own gym. And when things went darker, we stopped the fights being from competing gyms.'

'And what, you're just going to jump and end it like this? You give me names and I can get you in a protection program. There's ways to do this, Gordon.' Macleod felt a desperation inside because the man was coming clean to him in too quick a fashion. He had called for Macleod and now that he was here, the man was not hanging about with his confession.

'There's nowhere to hide from these people; some are in places you don't want to know. Besides, Macleod, I'm done in. I thought with the money that came from these fights, I would handle the guilt of sending some of these boys to their deaths. But I can't. If you look into the suspected drug overdose cases and other self-inflicted deaths around here, you'll find some of our guys. Not many; we only had one fatality a night and we only fought every two months or so. You can't draw too much attention after all.'

'So why did you let Kurt Eiger come over with our officer? I don't understand if it was all so good and quiet, why did you bring him?'

'All went off the rails, Inspector, when Kieran was killed. He was working for us but we didn't get rid of him. The boy was good as gold. Loved himself and thought he was a ladies' man but when it came to work, he was good. His death was a shock and being so close when it happened, I told Sonny to keep his head down.'

'Is that why Sonny ran when I called on him, he thought I was coming for him?'

Gordon shook his head. 'He ran because he thought you would attract them to him. You see he was watching when you were at Fischer's house, Inspector, and he called me. He reckoned you were there to start telling him I was dead, and they were coming after us all. Sonny was a good lad, but he was thick as two planks. I should never have brought him into it as he always looked over his shoulder when there was no danger at all.

'That night when Sonny told me about you being at Fischer's and I told the ones above me, they ordered a kill on Eiger and your girl. When she escaped, we got told to get her back. We didn't so I was told to eliminate the boys and then I know it will be my turn. This way I do it before they get me.'

'And you got to Fischer too?'

'Not me, Inspector, and I don't think it was us. They were surprised.'

'Think it over Gordon. I can get you away.'

Gordon Stones turned around and smiled at Macleod. 'It's okay, Inspector. I have a boy I never see and a wife that hates me. But today they will be looked after. The rest of the money is in the accounts of the Trust. I started out looking to help these boys and that's what I have ended up doing. And there's no more secrets and cover ups. No more of those kids dying a bloody death. I'm free. You'll find the others soon enough who were with me. Oh, and, Inspector.'

'What, Mr Stones?'

'Merry Christmas!'

Macleod realised what the comment meant and threw himself at the man standing on the wrong side of the railings, but he was away before the Inspector could grab him. Macleod did not look over as Stones fell but he saw the rope tighten and then heard the sickening crack.

There was no other option than to drag Stones back up quickly as they could but when they hauled him over the top of the railings, he was clearly dead. His Santa hat had disappeared, and his beard was at a jaunty angle. Macleod sat down on the cold pavement inside the railings and hugged himself tight. An officer put a hand on his shoulder and asked if Macleod was okay. He shook his head but then stood up and began to walk away. Then he turned and stood at the railings, looking out at Inverness.

'Sir?' It was Ross.

'What is it, Ross?'

'What are you doing?'

'He chose this as his last view. Why would he do that? A last look over a city. I mean he could have chosen anywhere to die but he chose here.'

'A place to make his last confession, sir. At least it's over.'

'No, it's not, Ross. He confessed to only the death of Kurt Eiger, and a few others we don't know about. He categorically denied to me killing Kieran Magee and Angus Fischer. We still have killers out there. And if we don't find Sonny King soon, I think he'll be joining them too. Get the car, Ross. Looks like Christmas has only just begun.'

Chapter 21

'Where to, boss?' asked Ross.

'Mrs Haskins's house. There is some unfinished business there.'

'I'm not following, sir.'

Neither am I, Ross, thought Macleod but he knew that something was bothering him about Kieran Magee's murder. His mind still had Kylie Magee as a suspect and his instinct was that she did it, but he had no proof. The first murder was incredibly open in terms of who could have committed it. Although there had been CCTV footage of who was around there was no definitive way of knowing everyone who was at the garden centre. Ross had gone over the statements, but they could not isolate out who was at the Santa tent at the time.

The murder of Angus Fischer was different. The killer had turned up in a disguise and a theatrical one at that. What was it that Gordon Stones had said? Everyone at the fight had worn masks. Macleod had a thought.

'I said, "I'm not following, sir."'

'Sorry, Ross, but I need to make a call.' As Ross drove through the cold evening, Macleod rang Stewart's mobile hoping she would be awake. After several rings, he heard a weary voice.

'Hello? Sir, is that you?'

'Yes, Kirsten, good to hear your voice. Sorry I haven't called back but it has been busy. I need to ask you something. Gordon Stones has just hanged himself off the Kessock Bridge but before he died, he confessed to Eiger's murder and a few more. But he also said at the event everyone wore a mask. Is that right?'

'So Eiger's dead?' There was a pause and Macleod could hear Stewart sniff.

'Are you all right, Kirsten?' Silence. 'Kirsten, you okay?'

'Sorry, sir, it's just the man saved my life. I still had a hope he might live. Where did you find him?'

'We haven't yet but I don't doubt Stones as I think he was being truthful for once in his life. But I need to know, were the people present in masks?'

'Just about everyone, sir, except for the fighters and Eiger and me. Oh, and the staff serving. Was a way of keeping mouths shut who were working there. Everyone knew you so if you grassed up, they could come for you.'

'Was there anything distinct in the masks?'

'Well, not really except for one mask. Actually, it was more of an outfit worn by the MC. He would come on in a black cloak and a face mask.'

Macleod looked for the CCTV footage of the masked shopping centre killer on his phone. 'I'm sending a picture, Kirsten. Tell me if this is the outfit.'

It took Macleod over two minutes to manipulate the mobile and then Ross to take the mobile and assist. But once the image was sent, Macleod could tell he was onto a winner.

'That's him, that's the MC. I didn't recognise the voice.'

Macleod pondered for a moment. 'Was the MC there the whole time of your visit?'

'Pretty much, sir as I remember but I can't trust all my memories fully as the cold really got to me. But I believe so.'

'Thanks, Kirsten, get well, and good work. Glad to have you back.'

'Well, that's us just about here, sir,' announced Ross, pulling the car over to one side. Macleod had been so immersed he had not even noticed the man starting the car again after his intervention with the picture on the mobile.

'Just a second, Ross.' Macleod wondered about the outfit. If Stones had been the MC at the fight, it was highly unlikely that he would have had the time to get to the shopping centre and back. And he also said he hadn't committed the crime. Dermott Haskins, however, had no real alibi, having been out at Dalmore House. He had gone to sleep for a while. So maybe he could have gone, made his way back quietly, committed the murder, and then been back at Dalmore. But it was very opportunistic. Macleod was not convinced.

'Sorry Ross, I'm just thinking about that outfit worn by the shopping centre killer. It matches one worn by the MC at the fights. Seems a bit crazy, a bit flamboyant to run around wearing it. If Dermott Haskins killed Angus Fischer, it would have been very spur of the moment. And why would they not send Stones to do it if it were to do with the fights? Apparently, Sonny King saw us at Fischer's but there was also someone outside the front. I remember thinking someone was watching.'

'And that all means what, sir?'

'I don't know, Ross. What I do know is we are about to find a lot of bodies as this fight organisation is closing down their operations. But we might lose our other killers if we don't keep our eye on the ball. Let's go see Mrs Haskins.'

Stepping out into the frosty air, Macleod saw the sky begin to darken. It would soon be night and from the cloud to the north, he reckoned they could be on the receiving end of another bout of snow. Macleod knocked on the door and stepped back while he awaited the opening of the door.

About two minutes later, the door opened with Mrs Haskins dressed in a white jumper and smart, chequered trousers. She had flour on her fingertips.

'Busy, Mrs Haskins? I am sorry to disturb you, but I was looking for Hughie.'

The woman smiled and raised herself up on her toes. 'I'm not in the habit of keeping my pets around all the time, Inspector. I did think about it with the trouble Dermott is in but then if a story broke and we got reporters, well . . ., you know how that could look. Besides, I have work to do tonight. What with all the Santa grottos being investigated, we have had a few cry offs and there was a party scheduled for children tonight. I can't get hold of Mr Stones and well, I wouldn't trust any of those criminal types, so I'm afraid Mrs Claus is making an appearance.'

Macleod nearly choked. 'Forgive me, ma'am, I realise that your husband and you may not be that close but he's up to his neck in drugs trouble. And you are attending a party for children. Why?'

'Dermott's niece is among the little ones, or so I'm told. The organiser called me this afternoon, for seven o'clock this evening. Short notice but it is better that Auntie turns up rather than no Santa. Sometimes you cannot have the kids thinking bad of their family, even if Uncle was playing *naughty boys and cruel women* with a teenager.'

'Have you seen Hughie since yesterday?'

'I'm afraid not, Inspector.'

'It seems that Hughie was in a bit of bother. He was seen at an illegal fight by an officer of mine.'

'But when, Inspector? I can assure you he was with me throughout the night. You even interrupted us, remember? Are you sure it was Hughie? He does have a twin brother, Inspector.'

'A twin? Has his brother even served time at Her Majesty's pleasure, Mrs Haskins?'

'Not that I am aware, but he is a naughty boy. I often wondered what it would be like having twins staying with me, but I think Danny is a lot more violent than Hughie. Maybe that's why he's never been caught.'

It certainly answered Macleod's question about what Hughie was doing at the fight. He did find it strange that Mrs Haskins was able to be in the house when he called at random. Given what she said, it would be hard to detain her, either at the station or in her house.

'Don't leave Inverness, please. I will need to speak to you again. Do you have a number for Hughie?'

Mrs Haskins walked inside before coming back with a mobile phone and holding the screen up to Macleod. 'I have been trying him Inspector, as Dermott's occupied, but I'm afraid his mobile seems to ring out. I do hope his brother hasn't got him involved in something.'

Macleod's mobile rang, showing Hope's image on the screen. 'Excuse me, ma'am.' Macleod turned away and answered the call. 'Hope, what's the matter?'

'We were looking for Eiger and someone made an anonymous call to the station about a warehouse just north of

Kessock. I didn't want to trouble you until we checked it out as it was a rather spurious caller according to the call handler. But when we got here, we found a winter wonderland with a number of Santa figures in various tableaus. Thing is, they are all dead.'

'Give me the address and I'll join you as soon as I can.' Macleod noted the information and then returned to Mrs Haskins. 'One final thing, ma'am. Did Mr Haskins have a cloak of some sort? Maybe a mask?'

'For what, Inspector, Halloween?' said the woman, laughing. 'Anything he had would probably be at his beloved garden centre. As you know he was quite the pervert and God knows what sort of games he got up to. Anything like that he would keep outside of the house. After all, I do have standards.'

Again, Macleod was taken aback. The woman had such an indignant way of talking about her husband when she was having sex with men in his bed. It was unnerving because you felt she might try to involve you at any time.

Back in the car, Macleod asked Ross to drive to the warehouse. In his mind he thought of this as a body count. Most of these people would have been dead for a while, certainly as soon as Stewart was found, or possibly before that. The decision to close operations and run had been taken at a high level and the only person left in the tangle was Simon Farrellsworth. Macleod believed that he would meet a sudden demise too. Or maybe he would make a run for it. Or already had. With the nature of who the man was, Macleod had left that particular tidying-up pleasure to his boss. The last thing the force wanted was Macleod facing a top-shot lawyer. And Macleod was not that fussed either.

Hope met the Inspector as Ross pulled the car into the

warehouse car park. From the outside, it looked like a normal warehouse but inside was a soft play that had been recently decorated ready for a grand Christmas party. The venue had been closed for the last two days awaiting an opening the following week.

Hope led Macleod inside and he was struck by the number of lights showing. There were soft play areas for children, each with a winter tableau. In one, Father Christmas was feeding his reindeer, but he seemed to have fallen to the ground. In another, Santa was climbing down a chimney but he seemed to have become stuck and was slumped over from the waist, his sack of toys lying on the floor. Another tableau had Mr Snowman smiling away while Santa sprawled on the ground. But the tableau that riled Macleod was one of a nativity scene, the baby Jesus with his mother and father and some angels watching over them. In itself, it was a rather crude but inoffensive picture. However, Father Christmas was sprawled on the ground with a glass of spilled wine or other liquid beside his beard.

'Is Miss Nakamura here?'

'It's kind of hard for Jona to keep up, sir, but Mackintosh is on scene. I believe Jona's looking at something in the garden centre with the drugs squad. Might interest you, she said, but she didn't want to tell you until she had something. Macleod nodded and then saw the stumpy white coverall of Hazel Mackintosh.

'Not the most festive scene I've ever witnessed, Inspector, but I guess this will bring the incident to a close. I have sent photographs of all the Santa Claus bodies to DC Stewart and she's identifying them now. I believe there are five fighters and three drivers.'

'Eight dead, Hazel; how do you kill eight people and then have them pose as Santa? Look at some of them, they are big lads. Not easy to do. Maybe simpler to just have a kill order unless you think we don't know about the kill order.'

'I'm not with you, Inspector.'

'Of course not, Hazel, you don't know the whole story. The man on the bridge that recently jumped to his death, Gordon Stones, confessed to me about the fighting ring and that a kill order would be going out. Ironically, he chose to die as Father Christmas. He must have known what happened here. He said as much, so he died in red too. But who did it?'

'Sonny King, I mean, we are still looking for him, are we not?'

'If you ever met Sonny King, Hazel, you'd know that this is beyond him. A proper thug and that but this took sophistication. We're talking eight dead. Any ideas how they died?'

'We need to get a proper toxicology report done but my guess is they were drugged, firstly with something making them suggestible and then something to kill them. I mean, look at them, Inspector, all neatly in position to a point, except they have collapsed. The one with the glass might be the exception. I think there's a blow to the head—it is rather caved in. Maybe the substance wasn't strong enough for him.'

Macleod thanked Mackintosh and asked her to keep him updated if anything new came to light. He fielded a phone call from his boss next, standing outside in the cold to keep the conversation away from the others. The hunt for Simon Farrellsworth was not going well and the man seemed to have fled the country.

'I'll drive this side of things,' said his boss. 'Does this end the

Highlands involvement, Macleod?'

'I don't believe so. There are a lot of bodies but I'm not sure everyone in the fight ring is accounted for.'

'How come, Macleod? This warehouse find puts the body count at ten.'

'And we still have Sonny King out in the wild. We also have two bodies without a murderer attached to them.'

'And how do you not know that they were caught up in this ring. As I understand it, Kieran Magee was a fighter, like Angus Fischer. Are you just seeing wood when they aren't even trees? Bring Sonny King in, Macleod; it looks like he could be the hitman for Mr Farrellsworth.'

'I strongly doubt that, Chief Inspector. The man is a thug but no hitman. But I'll keep on it. If we don't wrap this end up soon, there will be nothing to close. Just a few more dead bodies.'

Macleod for the life of him could not see the final piece as he sat on the cold step of the warehouse, drinking a coffee brought by a uniformed officer. Macleod thought the man deserved a medal, or at least a promotion as his hands were so cold. Hope joined him, dressed in her jeans and jacket as if there was a mild breeze on and not a cold winter's night.

'I've called the search off, obviously. Mackintosh says the only body in the warehouse that was dead beyond today was Eiger. He was still dressed up as Santa Claus though. Probably how the rest were brought here. Told they needed to get rid of him and then have a celebration before everything was broken up. But Gordon Stones didn't come, or he did and knew to duck out. Anyway, my money's on Dermott Haskins being involved in this ring too, beyond the drugs. I reckon he must have been there at Fischer's when you were there with Ross.

Then he went and killed Fischer.'

'I had a similar thought but something's not right, McGrath. Dermott Haskins did not do this. And Sonny King's not capable. And Stones didn't do it either. If he were going to kill himself, he would have let them run. He did have at least respect if not a love for his fighters.'

Macleod was interrupted by his mobile and he saw it was Jona Nakamura.

'Miss Nakamura, Mackintosh advised me you were helping the drug unit at the garden centre. I feel up here is somewhat more juicer but then again, they are not going to go away.'

'Sorry, Inspector, but they were looking for evidence down here and wanted things handled properly before they ripped them apart. However, you will be interested in this. In Haskins's personal safe was a mask and a cloak. It's identical to the one we saw on the CCTV at the shopping centre. It seems Dermott Haskins was on the move the night he claimed to be at Dalmore.'

Overhearing the call, Hope smiled at Macleod. 'So, Fischer was killed over the drugs.'

'No, Hope, he wasn't,' said Macleod, staring off into the night. 'Jona, are there any staff there at the moment in the garden centre?'

'Yes, the general manager, Mr Haskins's number two, is here.'

'Put him on, please; I'd like a word.'

Macleod heard a shuffling of the phone and then a quiet voice came on. 'Hello, it's Devon McDuff here; who am I speaking to?'

'This is DI Macleod, Mr McDuff. The personal safe of Mr Haskins that has just been opened. Was Mr Haskins the only one with a code to it?'

'None of the staff have the code, sir. It was not a work safe but one for Mr Haskins's personal things. I do believe that his wife may have known the combination. I'm sure I have seen her in the safe before.'

'Thank you, sir.' Macleod closed the call and stood up. 'McGrath, get the car. And what's the time?'

'Approaching seven o'clock, sir.'

'Come on, there's no time to lose.' Grabbing McGrath's arm, Macleod started for the car.

Chapter 22

'Where to, sir?' asked Hope.

'The station. We need to get hold of Eleanor Haskins. She's off to a kid's Christmas party dressed as Mrs Claus. She killed Angus Fischer. I'm sure of it—and probably everyone in that warehouse. They were brought along to get rid of Kurt Eiger and then Eleanor Haskins drugged them in celebration before setting them up as Santas and killing them.'

'How do you make that out?'

'The killer in the shopping centre wore a cloak and a mask which Stewart has identified. Now on the night, Gordon Stones was in the outfit at the fight. But there was a second outfit in the safe at the garden centre. Dermott Haskins usually wore it, but he was at the lodge asleep. It was a tough ask for him to make his way back, kill Fischer, and then return. Also, he had no way to know that group was going to be late. However, Eleanor Haskins knew her husband would be out. All she needed was someone to give her cover. Hence Hughie was at the house. She popped out with Hughie as cover for her and then killed Fischer. But she used the mask and cloak as cover.'

'Okay, so say you're right, Seoras, where is this party?'

Macleod grimaced at Hope. 'I don't know. I'm banking on Dermott Haskins helping me solve that issue.'

The pair sat in silence as Hope raced along the A9 back to Inverness, lights flashing atop the car. Then she turned to Macleod.

'What about Sonny King? If you're right, Eleanor Haskins has been mopping up, closing off all who knew about the illegal fights and the drugs to protect those higher up the chain. He was close to Gordon Stones, so he probably knew a lot.'

'And that's why he ran. He thought getting arrested by us would put him in the situation where they had to know he would not speak. He was not the cleverest, but he knew how the top feeders in this kind of organisation think. So, he ran. And that's why Eleanor Haskins is still here. The job's not finished.'

'And she killed Kieran Magee because he was involved in the ring too.'

Macleod shook his head violently. 'No, no, no! Think, Hope, come on. She came to me about having the affair with Kieran. Why? She wanted the attention away from herself, putting onto her husband if necessary. Not because she was the killer. If that was the case all she had to do was sit tight. No, she wanted distance between that killing and the ones she was about to do. Therefore, she admitted her role. She knew we were investigating Kieran's death and thereby his connections. He was involved in the fight scene.

'She tailed us and saw Ross and me at Fischer's house. And then having seen someone kill a *Santa in a grotto*, she saw the chance to make this look like something else. A serial killer. But we got into the fight scene fully and she got the word to collapse it. Permanently. I doubt she knew about the drugs her husband was involved with, because she would have disposed of them and kept herself and her husband clear. But she wore fight MC garb to keep herself secreted and to link it back to Stones or her husband if necessary.'

'So, what happened to Kieran Magee?'

'I can't prove it, but I told you my instinct is Kylie Magee.'

Hope turned the car into the station car park and Macleod was out of it and running for the building before she could remove her seat belt. Racing through the building, Macleod made his way to the drugs team on the second floor and burst through their office door, much to the surprise of the gathered team.

'Inspector Macleod, can I help you?' said a slightly over-weight black-haired man at the front of the room. Before him was a large number of detectives and uniformed officers who had all turned around in their seats to see who the loud intruder was.

'Inspector Sullivan, I need a word with your suspect. Where's Haskins?'

'Down below,' said Sullivan, pointing down with his finger. Macleod recognised he meant the cells and tore back out of the room. He nearly clattered into Hope as she finally caught up with him and he grabbed her arm, shouting, 'Cells, Hope, we need the cells.'

Macleod's breath had started to fail him at the top of the stairs on his climb up to the drug unit. Now he was running on empty as he careered down the stairs. Hope overtook him and when he made the holding cells, Macleod found Hope calmly pointing the way to a duty Sergeant with a chain of keys.

After leading the detectives to a plain door amongst many other plain doors, the Sergeant opened it and swung the door back. Inside Macleod saw Dermott Haskins on a bench leaning up against the wall. On the ground lay an uneaten dinner and he seemed white.

'Have they come yet?'

'Yes, they have, Mr Haskins,' said Macleod, 'and Mr Stones evaded them by throwing himself off the Kessock Bridge. But I need to shut down the killer. I believe your Eleanor may be at risk.'

The man started. 'Why would Eleanor be at risk?'

'Sonny King is still at large. I spoke to your wife today and she said she was going to your niece's Christmas party. I need to know where it is, so I can reach her. Would you know where it would be?'

'No, no! But my sister would. Contact Mary. She'll tell you. She'll probably have told Eleanor.'

'The number, sir?' asked Hope. Haskins rhymed off a number he was well used to. 'Thank you; we'll get her, sir.'

As Macleod and Hope left the cells, Hope nudged her boss with her elbow. 'Very clever, sir, and you almost didn't lie.'

Macleod turned with a look of annoyance. 'I did not lie one iota in there.'

'You said she was at risk.'

'She is. That's the point. Ring the sister and find out where we are going.'

Macleod stood and listened to his junior partner asking for the details of the party and heard a quizzical voice on the other end of the line. Hope asked the question again, but she seemed confused by the answer. When she hung up the call, Macleod looked at her expectantly.

'So, what's the deal?'

'Her sister said the party was an hour ago, but Eleanor

never showed up. She said that she never spoke to Eleanor directly—instead she spoke to a man. She called last night. Twice.'

'When Hughie was babysitting the house while Eleanor was off doing whatever she needed,' said Macleod, his face a picture of revelation. 'I think Hughie was friends with someone. Someone who used to be in the fight circle. Get Haskins and tell him we need to take him home.'

Macleod stepped out of the building as she waited for Hope to organise Haskins's temporary release. It was a shot in the dark bringing Haskins along but if Eleanor was really playing along at being the goodly wife she would have somewhere to make an obvious note of what she was doing, a form of evidence that she was taking care of business as a housewife. At least that was Macleod's hope.

Within ten minutes, Macleod was sitting in the back seat of a police car with Dermott Haskins. Two uniformed officers were in the front and Hope was following in her car. Trying to keep an even demeanour, Macleod ventured forth on a topic of conversation.

'How long have you and Eleanor been married?'

'What? Oh, five years. She's an old horse but she could turn a head when we first met. We met at a party thrown by this London lawyer; he owns the lodge. I've never met him since then, but Eleanor's been a good girl, introduced me to a lot of good deals, helped me get the garden centre. She didn't know about the drugs, just a good housewife.'

He doesn't even know, thought Macleod. *His wife's the enforcer up here for the group and he doesn't have the slightest clue. It must have been a plan all along. If we can get her, the DCI might be able to get some of the upper echelons.*

'Has she been faithful?'

'What sort of a question is that? Of course, she has.'

'Just wondering as you clearly haven't been, sir, so wondered if she played about too. I know some modern couples are not exclusive—I think that's the terminology.'

'Not Eleanor, solid little housewife. But sometimes I need a younger touch, something you can play about with. I'm sure you understand me.'

Macleod nearly went for him. But the Inspector required the man to get his real prize of Eleanor Haskins. 'Do you know Kylie Magee?'

'Not really, Kieran Magee's wife. I only saw her once when she came to pick up Kieran after the initial interview for the Santa job. She was a feisty soul. I remember her and Eleanor giving each other daggers. I think she was upstaging Eleanor. Was wearing those leggings the younger girls wear, Inspector, and a nice top if I remember. Yes, I did enjoy, but she looked like a wild one to handle.'

If the man made any comment about Hope, Macleod was not sure he would contain himself but what he had said about the two women was interesting. Kylie Magee had always said she was uninterested in Kieran after their initial years of marriage, but it seemed that Macleod's instincts had been right all along.

The car pulled up to the house and a handcuffed Haskins was brought to the front steps where Hope opened the door with the man's keys. Stepping inside, Macleod noted the tasteful wallpaper and neat house with not an item out of place. A picture on the wall had the Haskins staring into each other's eyes and Macleod could not help but be impressed with Eleanor Haskins's commitment to her role.

'Does she have a diary?' asked Hope.

'You could try the little drawer of the telephone table. She's always stuffing things in there.' Hope opened the drawer and began taking out a number of pens and pieces of paper before finding the leather-backed book Haskins was speaking of.

Hope opened the book and turned to today's date. 'Seven o'clock,' said Hope. 'Kaney Hall?'

'It's on the way to the airport,' said Haskins. 'Like an old scout hut but you can hire it. Not sure I've seen it being used lately. Thought it was a bit run down for a party.'

Macleod advised the uniformed officers that they should take Mr Haskins back to the station once they had locked the house. By the time he had completed his explanation, Hope was already back in her car and had the door open for Macleod.

'Do we bring back-up, sir?'

'We're walking in to try and take down a known killer and also someone who I believe used to be an MMA fighter. We haven't even got Stewart with us, Hope. Yes, we bring back-up. But silent approach, and we can't wait for them. Eleanor Haskins is our ticket to get after who really ran this fight ring and drugs from London. Let's go, Hope, but make sure you have something to hand when we go in.'

Chapter 23

Hope took the shore road towards the airport, a place often neglected by tourists and those requiring air passage as it was a more winding and laborious road. Other locals liked it, as they saw it as the better drive and a lot quieter. Certainly, no queues. At the early stages of night, the road was quiet, and heavily gritted. But snow falling again and a wind picking up made Macleod believe the authorities had not judged the weather correctly.

Macleod checked the map on his phone as Hope drove, scouring the sides of the road for the old scout hut. There were few lights about and only the occasional house making identification through the snowfall difficult. But up ahead, a car could be seen switching off its lights and a woman was making her way into a lit hut. From this distance, the woman seemed to be dressed in red.

'Up ahead, Hope. Where that car stopped.'

'Saw it,' said Hope and drove the car past the parked vehicle. Stopping a few metres further up the road, the pair exited the car and Macleod pulled his coat up around him. He had been running on work mode, something he did from time to time. Whenever something shocking or disturbing happened, he would shove the image to the back of his mind and simply keep going with procedure, or some degree of method designed to keep any regrets or horror at bay. Right now, work mode was struggling to dominate.

He had seen Gordon Stones throw himself to his death and had been unable to stop it. The tableaus of death in the soft play had chilled him more than he cared to admit. How someone could simply dispose of so many people at once horrified him. And his error at judging the risk to Stewart in allowing her to go undercover was shaking him to his core. Now he was putting Hope and himself at risk for what? To stop a murder, said his core. But this would be the murder of a cold-hearted killer, by someone she had wronged. He threw the conflict behind him again and tried to focus on the task ahead.

Hope crept ahead, making her way to the front door. Macleod saw her look in through a frosted window. 'I think there's two of them, sir.'

'Scout round the back and see if you can come in from that side. I'll go in and see if I can get their attention. Make sure you're quick about it, McGrath.'

Macleod had no idea just how dangerous this tactic would be. What would he find? Someone in the act of killing? Or had he misjudged, and he would face two attackers without his sidekick. No, he trusted his instincts; he had called this from the start. Macleod opened the door and saw Eleanor Haskins looking at him, shocked.

'Really, no need to follow me—'

Before she could finish, Eleanor Haskins was grabbed from behind by a smaller woman. The arm snaked around Eleanor's throat and Macleod saw her tense as the hold was swiftly applied. Soon, Eleanor collapsed to her knees and Macleod could see the face of Kylie Magee.

'Don't do it. We need her, Kylie. She's killed a lot of people, ruined your life. She needs to pay.'

'She'll pay,' laughed Kylie and Macleod watched Eleanor clutching at her neck before her hands began to fall.

'Don't, Kylie,' shouted Macleod, desperately looking for Hope. But Eleanor began to slump in Kylie's arms. Macleod would have to try on his own.

As he went to step forward, the door behind Macleod was flung opened and a cry was heard. Macleod was shoved sideways and crashed hard into the hut wall. Barely able to keep his feet, he turned and saw Sonny King running forward and grabbing Kylie Magee, whose arms fell from Eleanor's neck. Sonny tried to lift Kylie away, but she threw a punch to his face and he reeled. But the delay meant Eleanor was able to crawl forward and Macleod tried to reach down for her, drawing his cuffs. But he was dazed and could not find the handcuffs in his rear pockets. As such, he absurdly bent forward and grabbed a wrist without doing anything else.

Eleanor snarled at him and leaning on one hand jabbed at him with an open palm causing Macleod to stumble and fall. As he tried to get back up, he saw the scuffle between Sonny King and Kylie Magee was in full swing with a third participant now in the fray. Hope's red ponytail was whipping around as she ducked here and there before being caught with a fist that sent her rocking.

Macleod struggled for his feet and his vison was blurred by his eyes watering. But he could see Eleanor Haskins stand on her feet, rubbing her neck. She took a look at the fight before her and watched Sonny King throw Kylie Magee away. Without hesitation, Eleanor grabbed Sonny's shoulder and using a small knife, she slit his throat from behind. The knife pocketed, she turned and ran out of the front door.

'Hope, call the ambulance, I'll get Haskins.'

Macleod tore out of the door and ran for the car. Slipping the spare key into the ignition, for they always carried one key each, he watched Eleanor drive off before spinning down a track that led towards the main road. Macleod was unsure if this track actually reached the main road, but he fired up the car and drove after her. In the snow, it was hard to make out beyond the car ahead and Macleod felt the bumps of the track they were on.

And then they were in a field. The car headlights lit up only white and he saw Eleanor start to turn her car around. Trying to cut her off, Macleod clipped the rear end of Eleanor's car and smashed his own driver's side headlight in the process, making his view darker. But he continued to spin the wheel of the car and despite the rear end sliding out, he maintained pursuit.

Macleod followed Eleanor's car back along the track they had come down, reliving the bouncing surface and fighting to see as the snow began to drive harder. A wind had picked up and a blizzard had started covering the car windscreen between bursts of the wipers.

Macleod thought he saw another car up ahead on the road that the hut was on. The car turned up the track and seemed to be accelerating. In a few moments there would be a head to head if no one reacted. Macleod hit his brakes but had struck them too hard and he began to slide. Ahead of him a collision was imminent.

At the last moment, Eleanor's car tried to veer but the two cars collided and spun across the track. Macleod threw his hands up as he slid into the collision. His airbag inflated and he was thrown forward into it and then back to his seat.

The world spun. Macleod put a hand forward but failed to grab the steering wheel and everything remained in motion. His ears felt like someone had stuffed a ton of cotton wool in them for the noise of the outside world seemed distant. Something dripped onto his lips and when he tasted, he recognised blood. Maybe it was his own. Sitting there, Macleod slowly watched his view start to slow down. He had to get out of the car. There had been an accident. Although this was not the movies, it was still best to clear the car lest something happen. More like a small fire than a massive explosion but where he was would not be safe.

His hand fumbled for the door and at the second attempt he was able to pull the handle. Swinging his feet out, Macleod fell out of the car and landed in the increasing snow. As the bitter cold of the white blanket hit his face, he found himself snapping back to reality, the fog starting to clear.

Looking up, he saw the other two cars, windscreens smashed and front grills in a complete shamble. Macleod stood up but could not see anyone in the cars. But off to his right, he saw footprints starting across the field and he turned to follow. In the distance he heard sirens. Before, he had wanted a silent approach, but Hope must have got through to them.

His footsteps were heavy and he fought to keep a balance as he ran, lifting his feet out of ever deepening snow. *Stewart would have been buried in this*, he thought. *Stop with the comments, stop berating yourself. Just get the women.*

Macleod was not shod for a snowy field and he felt the cold, melting snow running down his socks and to his feet. These days he felt the cold more than when he walked the beat and Jane had insisted on buying him thermal socks to wear which meant his feet sweated in the office. And now, when they might have been useful, his choice of shoe meant they had become soggy ice packs around his toes.

Everything ahead of Macleod seemed dark and if he did catch a glimpse of movement it was soon obscured by the falling snow the wind was driving into his face. Normally he wore his coat open, but he stopped his pursuit briefly to zip and then button it up. Although not overly warm, it was stopping the chill of the wind and he was thankful for that. In his mind, he prayed that Hope would be following him. Of the two women ahead, he could not think which he would rather face, Eleanor, the cold-hearted killer, or Kylie, the fighter who strangled her husband. Having seen those they dispatched, Macleod could not help but think of himself as cannon fodder for these women.

'You took my husband, you bitch.' The voice sounded wild.

'Which one was he?' came the cold and calculated reply.

Macleod increased his pace and came to a ditch with a hedge beyond it. He could see footprints to the ditch and a hole maybe a person wide. The twigs and internals of the hedge looked like they had taken a battering and he surmised this was where the women had gone. With a quick run up, he tried to clear the ditch but landed short and fell back into it. He lay in a mass of snow and mud but fought to lift himself back up, his coat now sodden.

Pulling at the grass deep in the snow for purchase, Macleod hauled himself up and through the hedge to the field beyond. He saw a copse and there beneath swaying branches stood the two women facing each other.

Eleanor Haskins made a stab towards Kylie Magee, a small knife in her hand, probably the one she had slit Sonny King's throat with. But Kylie simply stepped aside and slapped the arm away. Eleanor responded with another slash, but Kylie again stepped away before landing a punch to Eleanor's face and the woman reeled backwards.

'Stop!' Macleod had yelled with all the authority he could muster, and the women half turned towards him. Maybe they were expecting to see a line of officers sporting firearms or at least some squad of serious riot squad experts capable of mixing it with the best. Instead they saw Macleod, the older Inspector, his coat half covered in a muddy, snowy mess and Eleanor Haskins laughed. Kylie Magee did not crack a smile but warned Macleod, 'Stay away. She's mine. I need to do this and then you can do what you want, Inspector. But don't get in the way.'

Looking at the scene, Macleod wondered what to do. If he stepped into the fray, he saw the only real chance of his survival as the scenario where the women killed each other at the same time. He was outgunned, almost hilariously. Hope might have stood a chance, Stewart more so. But even then, it would be a risky option.

The women turned away and faced each other again, and Macleod saw them grapple. There was shouting and biting before Kylie managed to get her arm locked around Eleanor's throat. With her back to Macleod, he saw Kylie hanging on tight and the scrabbling arms of Eleanor Haskins.

Scanning around him, Macleod saw the bulge in the snow and ran to it. Plunging his hands into the cold, white powder, he located a large branch and pulled it from the covering. It was unwieldy and definitely not balanced as a weapon, but he had little choice as he saw Eleanor Haskins start to weaken. Running up behind Kylie Magee, he swung the branch for all he was worth and heard the crack on her skull. She dropped like a stone, slipping off Eleanor. The older woman fell forward and gasping, she started to crawl forward.

Macleod realised he needed to secure her quickly and dove for her. He landed on her back and she collapsed into the snow, but he failed to grab her arms. With surprising strength, she turned over and then grabbed Macleod's throat. He grabbed Eleanor's hands, pulling them off his neck, but she then swung a punch, catching his chin and sending Macleod backwards.

Landing on his back, he scrambled for purchase and tried to stand up, aware that she might jump onto him. But as he struggled to his knees, Macleod saw Eleanor Haskins running again through the copse and for another hedgerow. With what strength he still had, Macleod stood up and half ran, half stumbled behind the compromised Eleanor Haskins. The neck hold that Kylie had caught her in was taking its toll and she coughed as she ran, clutching her throat.

Macleod was impressed by his progress, although it may have been down to the injury Kylie had sustained on Eleanor and as they reached the ditch at the oncoming hedgerow, Macleod reckoned he was within touching distance. He dived forward swinging an arm at Eleanor's legs causing her to tumble down into the ditch. As Macleod landed, he slid on the snow and followed the woman. He tumbled, cracking his head on a part of Eleanor and then hit the ground with a thump.

He knew he had to react quickly, knew his life depended on it but Macleod was simply too exhausted. The car accident, the punch to his chin and now the pursuit had all taken its toll and he could do nothing else but simply lie there, the wet and muddy snow starting to seep through his hair.

At first, all he saw was a cloudy sky as he looked up. It was dark but there were small glimpses of the edge of cloud to break a starless view. But then Eleanor Haskins was kneeling over him.

'You've been a right pain, Inspector. My bosses will be delighted that I disposed of you. One of life's ironies really. You see I speak with a charming but dim-sounding accent and people always believe me to be harmless. But not you, you found out. And I had to kill Hughie and his brother, Inspector. They were entertaining. You've screwed this up royally for me. So, I will enjoy this.'

Macleod saw a small knife being raised and tried to throw up his hands. The knife came down and he turned over instinctively. The blade caught his shoulder, once, twice and then a third time as Eleanor Haskins whipped the knife back and forth into Macleod. When she spotted he had rolled slightly, she placed the knife between her teeth and turned him over, straddling him to keep him from twisting. Taking the knife from her teeth, there was no goodbye, no forlorn look, just a rage. Eleanor raised the knife.

Something flew in from the left-hand side and slammed Eleanor off Macleod and into the bank. The knife dropped and Macleod saw the new arrival standing and throwing a punch to Eleanor's head. The woman fell forward and a pair of handcuffs were slapped onto the wrists of Eleanor Haskins. A hand grabbed the knife and threw it up to the top of the ditch.

Macleod breathed deeply, his heart racing and looked at the red ponytail of Hope McGrath, swinging out behind her. Her face had the same scar on it he had seen for nearly a month and she simply stared at him. Her mouth was bleeding, and her face was looking pretty battered.

'They got you good, Hope.'

'I think they got you worse, sir.'

'But I was starting from a lower platform.'

Hope grabbed his arm and help Macleod to his feet. As he went to brush down his muddy and sodden coat, his arm screamed at him, the wound coming to the fore of his mind. But Hope simply grabbed him and held him tight.

'I got you, Seoras, I got you.'

'And you paid for it,' said Macleod, holding her back and looking again at her face.

'Stop looking at my face. It's going to be all right, bit beaten, and a bit scarred but we did it, Seoras. We got them.'

Macleod gave Hope a hug and then went to help her out of the ditch they stood in as help arrived. But his injured arm gave way, and he slipped and fell. Grabbing her arm with his good one, he took her back down to the mud. It was inappropriate and strange to any onlookers, but the pair burst out laughing.

'Always holding me back, sir.' Now that sounded like Hope. But his arm really needed attention.

Chapter 24

Macleod found holding the telephone with his left hand awkward and ended up placing it under his chin and cradling it in a peculiar fashion with his shoulder. He was not a great believer in a speaker phone as anyone could walk in on a conversation. His right arm smarted if he bent it for too long and Macleod preferred the pain of a sore neck to another night of poor sleep due to his arm.

It was not often that Macleod was dressed particularly well at work. Of course, he wore a shirt and tie but that was really a uniform of sorts, one the younger generation was changing but he felt uncomfortable parading around in a cardigan. An open shirt also looked ridiculous. Not that he didn't look a bit of a fool right now. Jane had picked the tie and the large motif of a grinch had made him scowl to which she said, 'That's perfect. You match!'

Jane was next door making a rare foray into the station, a place she chose to remain clear of. Macleod's work was often brutal and unpleasant, and Jane had seen first-hand what evil lurked in the world. That was enough and she decided that her place was firmly out of the policing world. But his was not. Recently she had made that clear. Jane had fallen for a copper and she would never ask him to give that up.

The other person on the telephone was his DCI and she was wittering on about how well everyone had done. No, that was a bit harsh, but tonight Macleod had no time for it. For once a meal had been booked at a local curry house and they were going to have a Christmas feast. He had insisted on the forensic team coming as well and with his own team and partners, Macleod believed there was some thirty people attending. Ross had even felt comfortable enough to bring his partner and Macleod had made a particular point of arranging the seating so the man in Ross's life sat beside the Inspector.

His dealings with those with a marriage some members of his faith rejected had not always been reasonable. He was trying but the baggage he had been brought up with had not been fully off loaded. But having known Ross for a while now, and liking the man, Macleod felt he had to make a better effort. They were his demons to overcome; others should not suffer.

The bright side of his conversation with his boss was that they had begun to work the trail to those who had set up the fighting ring and who brought men and women to it—those who found death to be a sport. After his team had apprehended Eleanor Haskins, things had been passed up the line for investigations in London and other parts of the country. There were similar venues that were closing quickly, and a task force had been assigned. But Macleod was glad to be out of that.

The injured arm had given him time off work as he healed and although he had kept a watchful eye, he tried not to come in too often and make Hope feel he was watching over her. If she needed help, she'd come; he knew that now. And her confidence had come back. Her swagger was back, and she looked the better for it.

The DCI wished Macleod a Merry Christmas and reciprocating, he placed the telephone back on its receiver. On the desk in front of him was a newspaper and he noted they were still carrying details about the case, mostly factually incorrect or suppositions but when was that not the norm? He had been at a rather testy press interview and the DCI had interjected when Macleod had been asked if his detectives had been committed enough given the number of people who were dead. Macleod had remembered Stewart's near death and his bottom had come of the seat before his boss had placed a hand across him and delicately handled the question putting the press man in his place. Macleod had never hit the press but some days it was sheer luck he had not gone full throttle at one of them.

'Are you done yet?' It was Jane, dressed up and ready to party as she had put it. Macleod was unsure how he felt having her in his domain but there was no way he was going to tell her to remain home.

'It was the DCI, love. I could hardly chase her off.'

'She happy?'

Macleod nodded and stood for his coat. It was a new one, thick lined but Macleod needed a hand to get into it. His arm lifted but not easily. It would heal but not before the year was out. Coat on, Macleod escorted his partner into the main office and announced that everyone should move out or there would be no dinner tonight.

Surprisingly, Macleod enjoyed himself, not something he did on party occasions, especially those of a work nature, and he was even coaxed to a nearby club and onto the dance floor by Jane. When the place kicked everyone out at one o'clock, Macleod stood in disbelief as Jane announced that everyone could come back to their house for a nightcap. But she was back to being Jane, he noted, after her scare. The bus crash had left her slower than she was, but she had full mobility. But it was how she had healed from the other incident that made him smile. The flamboyant woman he had been so taken with had for a while run away. Well, tonight, she was back with a vengeance.

Macleod had waved what he thought was the last taxi away at four o'clock. But when he walked back into the house and began to embrace Jane, she pulled away. 'I'm off to bed, I think you should go see your other woman.'

For a moment, Macleod panicked, thinking that Mackintosh had said something rash and was waiting for him, having offended Jane. But when he looked out of the rear patio doors of the house, he saw Hope, looking out to the Moray Firth. She was in her smart jeans and a fashionable top, but her jacket was not on her. Macleod checked his coat rack under the stairs and fetched her leather jacket. As he passed though the lounge, he saw a bottle of whisky and grabbed it with a tumbler. Once outside, he first placed the bottle on the table along with the tumbler and then poured a large measure. Taking her coat, Macleod attempted to place the jacket on Hope's shoulders, but it fell, and she turned and picked it up.

'You'd better watch that arm, sir.'

'Here,' said Macleod, handing over the tumbler. 'It's fine—they're all away, Hope; it's just us.'

'I don't understand one thing, Seoras. For a man that doesn't drink, where do you get the courage to stand up and dance in a conga like that? You were outside yourself tonight.'

Macleod pointed back to the house and towards his bedroom. A light had just come on and he saw a face peeking out from behind curtains. 'That woman there!' he shouted, pointing at Jane. 'She takes me beyond myself. You just don't see that side of me too often at work.'

Hope drunk some of her whisky. 'The good stuff.'

'I wouldn't know. Someone bought me it. Clearly, they don't know me.'

'I'm not sure many do. How did you know there was more than one killer?'

Macleod yawned. It had been a long day and he was not feeling sharp. 'I didn't at first, not really. I thought Kylie was involved with it all. There was something about her. For all her talk and cover when we first met, I could sense it, her anger, maybe. I don't know, Hope; it's just how I click. Stewart has it too. You can't learn it.'

'I hear that they are going to trace just about everyone through Eleanor Haskins. Get some big names in industry and that, some celebrities who attended too.'

Macleod nodded. 'The DCI says so.'

'Bet you're popular.'

'I am, for a change. But Hope, I nearly screwed this up. Stewart's predicament could have been avoided. I didn't read that at all. It was poor on my part. At Fort Augustus, I did everything right, or rather we did, and we were the bad guys still. Now, despite nearly losing an officer, we are the toast. You don't get what you deserve—you just get what they want to give you.'

'You sound like it's not controllable.'

'It's not. Look at you. You act to save my Jane and you get scarred. That wasn't fair, but it was what it was. You couldn't control it. But you can control how you react. I screwed up sending Stewart, but I went for them after, made sure we got them. You can't change what's done.'

'Gordon Stones found that out.' Hope supped more whisky.

'I almost felt for him.'

'He killed, watched his so-called fighters die for the pleasure of others. I don't see it that way. Anyway, I think you deserve some more praise than you got. Sonny King's alive because of you.'

Hope nodded but she was staring out into the Firth. 'What's up?' asked Macleod.

'Saving him meant we nearly lost you. I spoke to Ross about this. He felt the same way when Stewart was on her own in Newcastle and that girl nearly killed her. It made me think.'

'Be careful with that. Too much thinking and you'll need more of that,' said Macleod, pointing to the whisky.

'No, seriously, Seoras. I thought I was going to be too late. And I remembered the other night how when we first worked together, you said this was no job for a woman.'

'Yes, well, I might have a slightly different perspective now.'

Hope turned to Macleod and placed an arm on his shoulder. 'It's me you are talking to; you don't have to use the PC version. I know that however much you think of me, or Stewart, or even Jona or Hazel, you still think this job is no place for a woman.'

Macleod held up his hands. 'Sorry, it's true.'

'Well, I agree, Seoras, this is no job for a woman.' Macleod stared at Hope slightly taken aback. 'Neither is it a place for a man. I get you now. You're not the boy's club kind of man; you genuinely want to see us safe. And as bloody patronising as that is, I get your honesty. Because I don't want to see you in this job either. It's not a place for old people.'

Macleod laughed. And he saw Hope had not. 'What's up?'

'As funny as that is, it still leaves why we need to do this job, why there exists this filth we need to deal with?'

'Now you are talking religion and faith,' said Macleod, 'and as it's past four, I refuse to answer.'

'Because the old man's getting tired?'

'Because the old man doesn't know the answer. There's a sofa inside or if you can find a spare bedroom you are more than welcome to stay. As for me, my age, as you have repeatedly reminded me, is causing me to tire, so I will respectfully take my leave. Don't drink the bottle.'

Macleod made his way upstairs and quietly entered his bedroom. He saw Jane huddled up, as she liked to sleep, and he tried not to wake her. As he climbed into the bed, she pushed herself back into him and Macleod cuddled Jane tight, ignoring the pain in his arm.

"She okay, dear?" asked Jane.

"Better than me, love. A lot better than me."

Read on to discover the Patrick Smythe series!

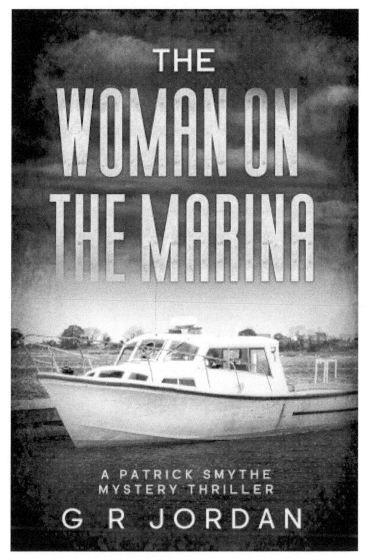

Start your Patrick Smythe journey here!

Patrick Smythe is a former Northern Irish policeman who

after suffering an amputation after a bomb blast, takes to the sea between the west coast of Scotland and his homeland to ply his trade as a private investigator. Join Paddy as he tries to work to his own ethics while knowing how to bend the rules he once enforced. Working from his beloved motorboat 'Craigantlet', Paddy decides to rescue a drug mule in this short story from the pen of G R Jordan.

Join G R Jordan's monthly newsletter about forthcoming releases and special writings for his tribe of avid readers and then receive your free Patrick Smythe short story.

Go to https://bit.ly/PatrickSmythe for your Patrick Smythe journey to start!

About the Author

GR Jordan is a self-published author who finally decided at forty that in order to have an enjoyable lifestyle, his creative beast within would have to be unleashed. His books mirror that conflict in life where acts of decency contend with self-promotion, goodness stares in horror at evil, and kindness blindsides us when we at our worst. Corrupting our world with his parade of wondrous and horrific characters, he highlights everyday tensions with fresh eyes whilst taking his methodical, intelligent mainstays on a roller-coaster ride of dilemmas, all the while suffering the banter of their provocative sidekicks.

A graduate of Loughborough University where he masqueraded as a chemical engineer but ultimately played American football, Gary had worked at changing the shape of cereal flakes and pulled a pallet truck for a living. Watching vegetables freeze at -40'C was another career highlight and he was also one of the Scottish Highlands "blind" air traffic controllers.

These days he has graduated to answering a telephone to people in trouble before telephoning other people to sort it out.

Having flirted with most places in the UK, he is now based in the Isle of Lewis in Scotland where his free time is spent between raising a young family with his wife, writing, figuring out how to work a loom and caring for a small flock of chickens. Luckily, his writing is influenced by his varied work and life experience as the chickens have not been the poetical inspiration he had hoped for!

You can connect with me on:

🌐 https://grjordan.com

📘 https://facebook.com/carpetlessleprechaun

Subscribe to my newsletter:

✉ https://bit.ly/PatrickSmythe

Also by G R Jordan

G R Jordan writes across multiple genres including crime, dark and action adventure fantasy, feel good fantasy, mystery thriller and horror fantasy. Below is a selection of his work. Whilst all books are available across online stores, signed copies are available at his personal shop.

 **Our Gated Community (Highlands & Islands Detective Book 10)**
https://grjordan.com/product/our-gated-community
A remote island community starts its new life. A dead body leads to locked doors and closed mouths. Can Macleod and McGrath find the killer hell bent on destroying paradise?

Leaving behind the city of Inverness, Seoras and Hope travel to the fledgling paradise of Morning Light to investigate a body found in the idyllic town square. When the Mayor tries to run roughshod over Macleod's investigation, the determined pair find a wall of silence and an underlying current of deceit and mistrust. Can Macleod find who controls the villagers' tongues before more permanent measures are taken against those who speak out?

A generous dose of fear is the key to a happy town!

Highlands and Islands Detective Thriller Series

https://grjordan.com/product/waters-edge

Join stalwart DI Macleod and his burgeoning new DC McGrath as they look into the darker side of the stunningly scenic and wilder parts of the north of Scotland. From the Black Isle to Lewis, from Mull to Harris and across to the small Isles, the Uists and Barra, this mismatched pairing follow murders, thieves and vengeful victims in an effort to restore tranquillity to the remoter parts of the land.

Be part of this tale of a surprise partnership amidst the foulest deeds and darkest souls who stalk this peaceful and most beautiful of lands, and you'll never see the Highlands the same way again

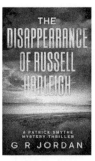

The Disappearance of Russell Hadleigh (Patrick Smythe Book 1)

https://grjordan.com/product/the-disappearance-of-russell-hadleigh

A retired judge fails to meet his golf partner. His wife calls for help while running a fantasy play ring. When Russians start co-opting into a fairly-traded clothing brand, can Paddy untangle the strands before the bodies start littering the golf course?

In his first full novel, Patrick Smythe, the single-armed former policeman, must infiltrate the golfing social scene to discover the fate of his client's husband. Assisted by a young starlet of the greens, Paddy tries to understand just who bears a grudge and who likes to play in the rough, culminating in a high stakes showdown where lives are hanging by the reaction of a moment. If you love pacey action, suspicious motives and devious characters, then Paddy Smythe operates amongst your kind of people.

Love is a matter of taste but money always demands more of its suitor.

Surface Tensions (Island Adventures Book 1)

https://grjordan.com/product/surface-tensions

Mermaids sighted near a Scottish island. A town exploding in anger and distrust. And Donald's got to get the sexiest fish in town, back in the water.

"Surface Tensions" is the first story in a series of Island adventures from the pen of G R Jordan. If you love comic moments, cosy adventures and light fantasy action, then you'll love these tales with a twist. Get the book that amazon readers said, "perfectly captures life in the Scottish Hebrides" and that explores "human nature at its best and worst".

Something's stirring the water!

Lightning Source UK Ltd.
Milton Keynes UK
UKHW010625010321
379583UK00001B/189